Had I Only Known

Had I Only Known

DADISI MWENDE NETIFNET

Had I Only Known
Copyright © 2019 Dadisi Mwende Netifnet

Cover Photo
http://creativecommons.org/licenses/by/3.0/

Cover Design by: Queen E. F. Phillips

Library of Congress Control Number: 2019919470
ISBN-13:   Paperback: 978-1-64749-019-5

All rights reserved. No part of this publication may be reproduced, distributed, or transmitted in any form or by any means, including photocopying, recording, or other electronic or mechanical methods, without the prior written permission of the publisher or author, except in the case of brief quotations embodied in critical reviews and certain other noncommercial uses permitted by copyright law.

Although every precaution has been taken to verify the accuracy of the information contained herein, the author and publisher assume no responsibility for any errors or omissions. No liability is assumed for damages that may result from the use of information contained within.

Printed in the United States of America

GoToPublish LLC
1-888-337-1724
www.gotopublish.com
info@gotopublish.com

Other Books and CDs by Dadisi Mwende Netifnet

Think With Your Spiritual Mind (Spiritual quotations)
Love Flows Like a River (Love quotations)
Poetry for Today's Young Black Revolutionary Minds
A Bachelor's Wish List
Sick People: The Things We Rather Not Talk About
Need I Say More
Upward Road (Autobiography)

CDs

I Saw Two Rainbows in the Sky | Cdbaby.com and Spotify playlist
Black Lives Matter: Spoken Words to Music pt. 1 & 2 | Cdbaby.com and Spotify playlist

you can visit my website *poetdadisi.com*
Youtube: Poet Dadisi

Contents

Dedication ix
Acknowledgments xi
Goodbye Houston 1
Hello Charleston 5
Home is Where the Heart Is 11
New Career 16
Distant Lover 23
Truly Adore You 27
I Think I Found My Soulmate 31
I'm On Your Side 41
My Prayers Are With You 44
When You Think of Me 47
Oh! How I Love You 55
You Open My Heart 62
Pull Me Up 72
Soaring Imagination 77
One Helluva Party 83
Searching for Answers 90
Things Begin to Happen 99

The Art of Survival 102
Let's Keep in Touch 107
The Restless Quest for Romance 116
Creating your own Challenge 120
On My Own 126
Mission Completed 132
On the Move 134
Present and Future 137
And That's Love 143
Forever Mine 147
Had I Only Known 153
About the Author 154
Other Books Written by Author 155

Dedication

I dedicate this book to my uncle, Felix, and Aunt, Grace Christian.

Thank you both for loving me unconditionally.

Acknowledgments

For the mother and daughter team, untold hours of editing and typing my manuscript-- my good friend Mrs. Wilma Adams and her daughter, who told me not to mention her name. Thank you from the bottom of my heart for making my dream book come true. Thanks to you, I have received much joy.

I am exceedingly grateful to God for bringing Queen Phillips into my life. She turned my novel, which has been sitting in my closet for eight years, into an e-Book in two days. I am grateful to God for your gift.

Thanks to Wanda (Mawiyah) Griffith for always being there to listen and help me clarify my ideas on paper. You mean a lot to me, and I salute you.

I also want to thank Mrs. Amanda for her expert input as the final editor of this book. Your effort is greatly appreciated. Thanks.

Special thanks to Kim Dupree who believed and encouraged me to write this romance novel.

Goodbye Houston

As Oleather walked out of the building that housed the People's Accounting Firm (PAF), she struggled with the last box of her personal belongings. Marvin was approaching the door; He had just finished eating lunch at the corner bar. "Ms. Chestnut, let me help you with that box." Oleather, with a sigh of relief, handed the box over.

"Whoa girl, this is heavy. You sure are a strong woman. Where are you going, to a meeting"?

"No, actually today is my last day working at this office. I'm being transferred to our other office in South Carolina so, I am taking the personal items I have accumulated over the past months to my car."

"What's happening in the Charleston office"?

"Oh, nothing major, just a little homesickness. I miss my family and friends. I've been here in Houston for nine years, and now, it is time to move on."

"I hear you, but you will be missed, girl."

Oleather looked at him as though she could not believe what she was hearing. "Really"!

"I think so," Marvin said as he followed her to her parked car in the reserved space outside the building.

"Thanks, Marvin, that's a lovely thing to say."

"I wish I could invite you out to dinner before you leave," Marvin said, looking a bit uneasy and surprised by his invitation.

"Thanks, Marvin, but my flight leaves at six in the morning, and I've got a thousand things to do before I leave town." Oleather wondered about Marvin's sudden obvious attraction. She had often seen Marvin in the office and had said an occasional "hi, how are you" in passing, but she contained her feelings. Marvin was a fine brother in his early thirties like Oleather. She had fantasized about being close to him on many occasions. He was about 6' 2" with chiseled features, a nice ass, and it was obvious the brother worked out. Marvin always seemed focused in the office; he had a good reputation for his professionalism.

"Let's keep In touch"? Marvin asked.

"That will be fine. After you help me with the box, I'll write the telephone number down where you could reach me in Charleston." Oleather stood in front of Marvin, and then she turned around and bent over in her mini skirt to put the key in the trunk to open it. Marvin was sizing her nicely shaped legs and butt. He also secretly fantasized about what it would be like seeing her with all her clothes off. Now would be his last chance to make that move. Oleather shut the trunk and turned to thank Marvin for helping her with the box. He was smiling at her, and she smiled back. "Oh yeah, let me give you my telephone number." Are you sure you're going to call me one day?" Oleather said while pointing her pen at him in a playful gesture.

"I'm sure." Oleather handed him a business card with the number on the back.

"Let me have yours too, just in case...." Marvin reached for his back pocket.

"No card, please, I'll write it in my telephone book; that way, there's not much chance of me losing it." Oleather got her telephone book from the front seat of the passenger side of her car, and Marvin exchanged her number for his. "Marvin, it was a pleasure working with you."

"The pleasure was all mine. Take good care of yourself, and don't be surprised to hear from me soon."

"You do the same." Marvin extended his right hand to give her a good-bye shake.

"Oh, Marvin," she said, "We can do better than that." She walked closer and gave him a big hug. Her embrace felt eternal. Marvin wanted to hold her longer and tight; then Oleather stepped back; she looked into his exciting eyes and asked him why he waited so long to ask her out to dinner.

"I was afraid," Marvin said

"Afraid of what"? She asked.

"Losing my job."

"Well, you don't have to worry about that anymore, now, do you? Call me."

"I will soon."

Oleather got into her car and drove off, feeling a throbbing between her thighs and wondering why Marvin waited so long to approach her; Things may have been different.

Marvin stood there until Oleather's car disappeared around the corner. He knew she was going, but in his mind, he definitely wouldn't forget her. He also was fighting an erection he thought would not go away any time soon. The attraction between them was definitely mutual. Marvin silently hoped this would go to another level.

Hello Charleston

"Dang girl, answer the telephone." Marvin fussed. Ring, ring, ring...

"Hello."

"Hi Oleather, it's Marvin. How are things at your end of the world? I thought you were asleep for a moment there."

"Hey Marvin, it's so nice to hear your voice. I was going to call you after I got through cooking dinner."

"I wish I were there to have dinner with you. What are you cooking"?

"Salmon fillet with red wine sauce, dirty rice, sweet peas, and salad."

"Hmmm, sounds delicious; maybe I can taste your hand next month when I come to visit you in Charleston"?

"You are coming next month? That's good news. I'll cook for you," chuckling, she teased, "I do aim to please, you know."

"Oleather, I wish I had met you long before the company transferred you to Charleston."

"Marvin, you met me more than once on the job. You just didn't pay any attention to me. Instead, you were pure business action, like an upper-class Negro."

"Okay, I guess I deserved that, but girl, you know when you are working in white corporate America, a brotha's got to fake it until he makes it…you know, kick-ass before you kiss ass." They both busted out laughing.

"Well, Marvin, just for the record, you don't need to fake it with me."

"I hear you, Oleather. By the way, guess what?"

"What?"

"I am going to be a Parole Officer for the State of Heartland."

"Parole Officer?" Oleather's voice lowered as though she had just been given some bad news. "You will be dealing with crazy-ass convicts. Don't you think that's going to be a tiny bit dangerous?"

"I guess, Oleather, but I am looking forward to the challenge."

"Well, you go ahead with your bad self. If that's what you'd like, I'll support you one hundred percent. Is there any money in that kind of work?"

"The starting pay is $35,000."

"You know, that's my beef with the State. It seems like they would pay a nigga' more than that a year for putting themselves on the line like that. All these fools I hear getting out of jail, child molesters, three-time murderers, and all the like. If I were a judge, I'd throw the damn key away and forget about those people. Obviously, it wasn't important to them to think about their actions; why show any mercy on them? They always know what they are doing or about to do is dead wrong. Why still do it? Maybe, that'd be a nice subject to complete my second degree in. I'll straighten some of this shit out."

"Oleather, you are a tough cookie girl. Too tough."

"You know, maybe I am, but that's what society needs. A tough black woman like me in their courts to help straighten this so-called system out."

"Well, since it's my job now to assist the parolees, maybe I can help someone turn their life around."

"Just don't be too light on their sorry asses. The taxpayers are paying you. Anyway, is that what you called me for Marvin? To tell me about your new job as a Parole Officer."

"Uh-huh, that, and to hear your sweet voice.

"You think I'm sweet?"

"Sweeter than coconut pie, and I love coconut pie. If you give me a chance, I'll show you. You like being frank, and I hope you don't get offended by me telling you that once I lick you over a few times, you will be so hot and wet your nipples will stand tall."

"Marvin, you are making me hot between my legs talking like that, and no, I am not in the least bit offended."

"It's all good, Oleather; it's all good."

"So, when exactly are you coming to Charleston to spend some time with me?"

"I'll let you know the exact date once I have confirmed my flight reservations."

"Sounds good! I can hardly wait to see you again. It seems like it's been a lifetime since I've seen you."

Laughing, Oleather said, "hang on, I guess I'll need to get my datebook to check my availability."

"What do you mean, datebook?"

"Chill Marvin, it's slang talk the girls use when their man is coming over to the house. By the way, is it safe to consider myself your lady?"

"That's another thing I wanted to talk to you about. You see, Oleather, I am a single man; I have no one in my life. I am neither bi-sexual nor gay. I am straight-up heterosexual."

"Tell me this, Marvin, do you enjoy cunnilingus?"

"What?"

"I think you heard me quite well. Do you want me to repeat myself?"

"Oleather, is that something you should be asking me?"

"I think so. It's a definite requirement as far as what I expect from my man."

"Girl, you sho' can put the pressure on a brotha."

"Well, if you can't stand the heat, don't think your ass is welcomed into the kitchen."

"Oleather, I think we need to have this conversation at another time," Marvin said nervously.

"Nothing's going to change my mind until you answer my question."

"What?"

"Do you enjoy cunnilingus or not?"

"Sometimes."

"How often?"

"I don't know."

"You know, alright. Do you enjoy cunnilingus before fucking or afterward?"

"Of course, before doing the wild thing. Girl, tell me the truth, how would you feel if I asked you a raw question like that?"

"Hell, I have no problem answering – I'll tell you straight up what you want to know. I'm sure, not afraid to tell my man what turns me on or off. Alright, putting all jokes aside, what is it that you really like and admire about me, Marvin? It's not like I'm in Houston anymore."

"I'm attracted to your carefree attitude Oleather, and I think you are a lot of fun to be with."

"I like you too, Marvin. I especially like your ass and those legs of yours. In my eyes, you are the complete package."

"Oleather, you sure are a force to reckon with."

"Now, where have I heard that before?" They both laughed.

"So, what about it Oleather, do you think you can stand to have a long-distance relationship with me or what?"

"I'm game, Marvin."

"Cool, then it's on. You for me and me for you."

"Marvin, I'm so happy you asked me. I have been thinking about you a whole lot lately."

"I am glad you accepted my offer, Oleather; you won't regret it. I'll be the man you need and deserve."

"Are you sure?"

"I'm sure."

"Have a good night, Oleather."

"You too, Marvin." As he placed the telephone back on the receiver, Marvin smiled to himself and thought, She will be a good woman for me. I better go get something to eat before I call it a night. I start my new job tomorrow. Some people call Monday "Stormy Monday," but I sure do hope it's not too bad for me. A new woman in my life, a new job; this is the life."

Home is Where the Heart Is

Charleston, South Carolina; the city of my wide-eyed introduction into this world. Whenever I come back to visit, I feel as if time stood still. All those skinned knees, climbing trees, kiss-n-telling, falling, getting up, being happy to be nappy, memories that I carry inside the treasure chest of my heart. Charleston, the place where I made my transformation from a girl into a full-fledged woman.

I am still evolving nonetheless, but the 3-D effect my experiences have had on my life, deflowering, developing, and defining, was ultimately critical to the success I now or ever plan to enjoy.

It's a warm and pleasant Sunday morning, my second week back in Charleston. I probably should have made it to church service, but I'm just so relieved to be finished with my move from Houston. Not to mention, I'm not in the mood for any family or mother's cackling friends. Hardly anyone knows I'm back home, and the news would be like notifying Smokey Bear about a forest fire. I'm shaking my head from side to side – I know it was the way I left home. I was in a hurry to get on with my life. Some people thrive on hearing the worst. I can imagine comments like, "that poor girl ain't gon make it," "is she okay – she's probably doing pretty bad."

I'm in the study room of my new apartment. Resting on my chaise lounge the color of cayenne pepper, head on my king-sized down feather pillow, and cover my chin with my favorite quilt. I'm taking mental stock of my present situation and how certain things have transpired. My chaise lounge was my gift to me the same day my divorce was final, my symbol of freedom. I feel inspired every time I lie on it. I once read that a person's name creates a special aura around them, making for a perfect fit.

Oleather Rae Ellis is my original name. T. Rae is now out of the question. Actually, I'm tickled about it now, but not in high school, though. I recall a particular incident in high school. I was nicknamed T. Rae up until then. Blockhead, class clown Trevor McDaniel had the nerve to ask me, very loudly during 5th period, if "T. Rae stood for big tittie Rae." If I were swift, I would have asked if Trevor McDaniel was an alias for "Trick Mac." Anyway, since then, T. Rae has been reserved for those closest to me.

Early in our marriage, Myles Ellis, my ex-husband, used to call me T. Rae his beautiful joy. To think I was deeply in love with this man. Myles was the love of my life. We met in college during my sophomore year, and we married one year after we'd both graduated from the University of Houston. I had this idea about how everything would happen at a specific time, and I suppose I did drag him down the aisle kicking and screaming at first. After a while, our lives picked up momentum on the tracks. Both of our careers were beginning to take off, so it was of no consequence to me that Miles worked an excessive amount of "overtime." We were like two ships passing; I realize now I was in denial when I played off his cold shoulder. There was a time when we'd see each other, and our clothes would go flying. Suddenly, he behaved like my body was hot volcano lava – our mattress sunk straight down the middle like cement in an earthquake.

It sure is funny how irony has a way of getting the last laugh. I'll never forget that day; it was an early afternoon in late September. Myles and I had been arguing the night before, which seemed to be our standard way of communicating for several months. It didn't dawn on me until after everything hit the fan that this was his grand scheme to make daily departures. I complained that we didn't spend time together anymore and that even dinner was a near impossibility. He shrugged his shoulders and swore around that it was because we didn't share the same interests. This flippant attitude pushed my buttons, and I started waving my hands in the air, hollering, "well, how in the hell did we get married if we were so incompatible?" I didn't really want an answer. I knew the truth. He stood there looking at me with his arms folded, forehead wrinkled, and mouth open like I was a scratched CD he could have sworn was in okay condition.

I took a super deep breath and said, "Okay, let's just go, let's just go somewhere and have dinner." To my surprise, he gave into defeat and suggested some out-of-the-way Chinese restaurant that he'd only "heard about." He knew I hated Chinese food, but I called his bluff. When we arrived, I immediately felt this strange vibe, and at the time, I didn't put two and two together when the waitress addressed him by his first name. On our way home in the car, he could tell that I'd felt sick to my stomach, and he had a smirk on his face as if to say, "Now, that's what you get, and don't ask me for anything else." Sure enough, I was as sick as a pregnant woman during early morning vomit sessions. When we got home, I headed straight for the bathroom, losing my dinner. Max went to bed without checking on me – as if nothing was wrong. I left for work the next day and had to turn around at about eleven forty-five to head home.

Our street sign was several blocks from our house, but we lived in a cul-de-sac so, I could see the house as I turned onto our street. I

Had I Only Known

made that right on Druid Circle and immediately felt that same vibe I'd gotten at the Chinese restaurant and on several other occasions, like when he'd disappear for hours after an argument. I was driving slowly, and as I was approaching from a distance, I was starting to make out a familiar car in our driveway – not mine or Myles. Once I got close enough, I read the personalized license plates, B.O.B. my heart started racing. It was one of my closest friends and bridesmaid, Roxanne. She was a very flamboyant individual – B.O.B. stood for Bitch on Board!

She was someone with whom I confided about my marriage, among other things. My adrenaline was pumping, and although my insides felt like mush, I was on a mission.

I got out of my car; I didn't even close the door or activate my alarm. I opened the gate to the backyard and went around to the utility room door that we kept unlocked, which led into the house. I knew to expect the worse, but I wasn't totally sure if I could handle whatever I was about to witness. I was on the prowl like a lioness ready to pounce. Instinctively, I began walking down the hall toward our bedroom, but noises were coming from the den. On my way there, I was starting to see a trail of clothes; a thong, matching bra, slip-on dress...I began to feel queasy, and then I could hear intense moaning and Mile's voice sounding deep and throaty, saying, "Oh baby, you're so wet." Mortified, I saw Roxanne bent over the armrest of our sofa stark naked in hooker red heels. Myles was clutching her by her waist from behind and pumping so fast and hard he didn't even notice me screaming his name until I chunked a candle holder at him, narrowly missing the back of his head and crashing violently into the wall. As I was slapping Myles all around his face and chest, Roxanne was stumbling to get to her clothes. I shouted all kinds of obscenities while Myles, with his penis still erect, was trying to fend me off and pull up his pants at the same time. I demanded he leave, and then I collapsed right there on the carpet. I don't know how long I had passed out, but I woke up to Myles asking me if I was okay. I started to scream again when he told me he was leaving. He should have just given me a swift push off an airplane without a parachute. I thought my life was over. I would come to learn that this was only the ending, making room for an unexpected beginning.

I snapped out of my reminiscent mode, got up from my chaise lounge, and walked to the kitchen to make some tea. I took a deep breath (something I often do) while staring at my teapot on the stove. I think, "Yes, this is where I belong." I'm not running but rather magnetically drawn to this place like a great winged bird to the highest skies. I attribute that to the fact that I am a survivor.

Once I visited Cardinal Mbiyu Chui, pronounced, bi-yu chu wee. Cardinal Mbiyu Chui was a minister at the Shrine of the Black Madonna Church in Houston. I wanted to refer to this chart called the Medicine Wheel. Cardinal Mbiyu described me as a person born of fire. His exact words, "you are the most quintessential form of a hot-headed strong-willed vixen," this chilled me to my bones. I was not to be mistaken with "one, born of water, but I was a humble soul full of resolutions and caution." Honestly, I probably need to be back here so that the peninsula can quench my so-called fire inside. Not to mention, I miss my family immensely. My parents Anna Mae and Elijah Ellis, are still holding down the fort after thirty-one years. Thirty Grove Street's white and greenhouse will always be home to my three brothers, five sisters, and me.

New Career

"Good morning, my name is Marvin Kenyatta, and I am the new Parole Officer."

"Hi, my name is Debra Jones, and I am the Clerk. Mr. Edmond, the Parole Supervisor, has been expecting you. Please have a seat, and I'll let him know you are here."

I thanked Debra. Debra seemed to be a nice enough person to work with; she was short and had a nice body. I could tell she did not take flak from anyone, though.

I was sitting in the lobby alone when four brothers and a white guy walked into the lobby about fifteen minutes later. They went over to the window and signed a white sheet of paper, and sat down. I heard one of the brothers telling the other that he doesn't ever want to go back to jail. He said it was no place to visit "over again and again." The other brother agreed and added that he would get his "shit" together this time around.

Debra came back to the window. "Mr. Kenyatta, you can come to the door; I'll buzz you in." I pulled the door open to the sound of the buzz and started walking down a long hallway when Debra yelled out to me, "Mr. Kenyatta, come this way, please." I followed Debra to Mr. Edmond's office.

The office was nice-sized. It smelled like Lagerfeld cologne. A bookshelf seemed to be overloaded with books, and the desk was crowded with paperwork. Mr. Edmond stood up and shook my hand. He was a medium-built black man with a serious expression on his face. "Good morning Mr. Kenyatta. Welcome to the parole department."

"Thank you, sir," I said.

"Thank you, Ms. Jones," he said in a monotone voice and asked Debra to close the door behind her. "Mr. Kenyatta, please have a seat. I understand that you have a Bachelor's degree as a Social Worker and a Masters in Finance."

"That is true, sir," I said.

"Do you have experience in both fields? If so, which of the fields do you enjoy working in the most?"

"I'll have to say Social work, sir," I answered honestly. Anticipating his next questions, I continued, "I enjoy working with people, the public. I feel as though I can contribute a lot towards society's needs in this arena." Mr. Edmond told me that as a Parole Officer, I would be working with many people, mostly "society's throw-offs," which would allow me to make a difference in someone's life. Mr. Edmond assured me after our lengthy conversation; he felt confident that I would make a difference in my new assignment. I was shown to my new office, Room 34. The small room had a desk, telephone, and a bookshelf.

"Make yourself at home, Mr. Kenyatta; we are glad to have you onboard." Once again, I thanked Mr. Edmond. Before I left his office, he mentioned that my officer training would start on

Thursday and, if I needed anything, to call him at extension 261. He advised that I utilize the next three days organizing my office and getting acquainted with the other officers.

I can definitely use more office space than this, I thought. But, if this is my new workplace, I had better make the best of it.

Lost in the familiarization process, I was rescued by a voice, "Hi, I'm officer Lee, your next-door neighbor; welcome aboard." Ms. Lee was a short, attractive woman of oriental descent.

"Pleased to meet you," I muttered, snapping out of my world. Ms. Lee offered to take me around for a grand tour to introduce me to the other officers in the building. I accepted the invitation, and before I noticed it, I was led from one office to the next, greeting and meeting officers from all walks of life. Female officers ranged in ages from the early '30s to the late '50s. This was going to be my first time working with so many blacks, not to mention a black woman holding the position of Regional Director. Her name is Miss Saye?? I think…She seemed to be very nice, but I was not going to take any chances, not yet anyway. I decided to get a feel of the place before I let my guards down.

I ventured back to my office and decided to start filling out my benefits package. As I remember, those can be a pain in the ass. I know I am going to need health and dental insurance coverage. Never can tell when I may become ill. All this paperwork will probably take me all day to complete.

My telephone started ringing, and I almost jumped out of my skin. I picked up the receiver and answered, "Mr. Kenyatta."

"Mr. Kenyatta," came the voice on the other end, "Mr. Edmond would like you to sit in with Ms. Lee on an interview in her office. Her office is on the right-hand side next to yours."

"Thank you," I said, "I think I remember where her office is, and we met a little earlier."

"Great!" she said in a cheerful girlie way and hung up. Guess I'll continue this paperwork later. I left to go to Ms. Lee's office for my first experience interviewing a parolee. This should be good.

"You come right on in, Mr. Kenyatta," Ms. Lee said, "make yourself comfortable. I am going to show you how to interview these knuckleheaded parolees. The first thing you need to do is establish that you will send their butts right back to jail if they mess up." She burst out laughing. "I know you must think I have lost my mind, talking like this, but seriously, you are here to enforce the rules and regulations of the State of Heartland." She handed me the parolee's records and stated that the documents must be kept confidential between the Parole Officer and clients at all times. "Mr. Edmond or your supervisor are the only few who can review your records at any time. Follow me to the lobby; that's where all parolees wait to be interviewed." She walked, and I followed.

A young Hispanic male, seemingly in his early 30's, was sitting alone in the lobby. His right leg was broken, and his forehead was pretty bruised up. "Whatever happened to you, Mr. Garcia?" Ms. Lee asked.

"I was involved in a car wreck this past weekend."

"Can you walk?" she inquired.

"Yes, Ma'am," he replied in a low voice.

"Follow me back to my office, Mr. Garcia."

We went back to Ms. Lee's office. "Please, have a seat, Mr. Garcia. This is Mr. Kenyatta, one of our new Parole Officers."

"What's up, Mr. Kenyatta?" I professionally greeted him.

Had I Only Known

Ms. Lee dove into her questioning session with Mr. Garcia. "Mr. Garcia, tell me in detail what happened to you over the weekend."

"I had a wreck," he said.

"Who was driving?"

"I was."

"Mr. Garcia, do you have a driver's license?"

"No."

"Then, would you like to explain to me why you were driving?"

"I needed to go to the grocery store."

"Couldn't you have gotten the owner of the car to drive you to the store?"

"He was drunk."

"Were you drunk too, Mr. Garcia?"

"I had a few beers."

"Sounds like you had more than a few beers to me. A few beers got you so drunk you almost killed yourself, Mr. Garcia? I think you had better leave those beers alone. Let me get you to do a urinalysis so that we can determine what you have been doing with yourself. Mr. Kenyatta, will you please take the cup and follow Mr. Garcia to the restroom? Mr. Garcia knows the procedure by heart. Mr. Kenyatta, your job is to watch and see that Mr. Garcia doesn't put any liquid or foreign objects into the cup."

"Sure," I replied.

"Thank you, Mr. Kenyatta. Mr. Garcia, I will see you back here in my office in a few minutes."

I followed Mr. Garcia to the restroom, opened the door, and let him into the restroom. Mr. Garcia expressed that he was "holding this piss for Ms. Lee for 20 minutes." It was obvious that he was relieved after emptying his bladder. He placed the cap on the cup and started walking towards the door.

"Aren't you forgetting to wash your hands?" I asked Mr. Garcia.

He laughed and said, "me, naw man, I didn't forget?" Yeah right! After he washed and dried his hands, I opened the door and led him back down the hall to Ms. Lee's office.

"Mr. Kenyatta, if you don't mind, would you please escort Mr. Garcia back to the lobby?"

"Not a problem, please follow me, Mr. Garcia." I offered. I escorted Mr. Garcia to the lobby and returned to Ms. Lee's office.

"Come in, Mr. Kenyatta; let me share with you the procedure for handling a case like Mr. Garcia's. First, how good are you with the computer?"

"I know my way around," I mused.

"Good," she smiled. "First, we are going write up a report for the analyst department in Austin. Mr. Garcia has committed several violations of the law. He doesn't need to be out on the streets. I'm going to let him sit out there until I find out what to do with him. Hopefully, after I fax this report to Austin, they will issue a warrant for his arrest. Come on, Mr. Kenyatta, let's go to the front office, and I'll show you where the machine is to fax the report." I followed Ms. Lee out of her office, down the hallway, and around the corner to a large reception area. There were five desks where three black females, one white female, and a brother were busy at work. Ms.

Lee introduced each of them to me. I shook their hands and told them my name. We walked over to the fax machine and faxed the report to Austin. After which, I followed her across the hall and to the break room. I offered to buy her a soda, to which she accepted. We engaged in some small talk. She wanted to know if I thought I would like the job, based on what I have seen so far.

"It's difficult to tell right now – I guess it's too soon," I said. "I am willing to give it my best shot, though."

"It really is not difficult. The most difficult part of this whole thing is the monthly payments. Do you have a part-time evening job?"

"No," I answered, wondering where she was going with this. "If you are good at budgeting your money, you won't have any problems; it's really a pain being paid once a month," she said, "However, if you are anything like me, and love to spend money, then you are going to need a part-time gig."

"I hear that." We sat in the break room for about twenty minutes before going back to the office where the fax machine was located.

The analyst in Austin had faxed a report issuing a warrant to have Mr. Garcia detained. Ms. Lee smiled at me. She said, "I just did society a favor. Mr. Garcia may not like it, but I'm doing him a favor too." We went back to her office. Ms. Lee then called the Houston Police Department for an officer to come to the Parole Office to pick up Mr. Garcia. Just as she hung up the phone, the urine technician returned with Mr. Garcia's test results. The results showed traces of marijuana in Mr. Garcia's urine. Ms. Lee was right.

Distant Lover

I wish Marvin was in town now that I know he enjoys cunnilingus. I would have invited him over to my apartment tonight to see if what he confessed was for real. A man's mouth will say anything until a woman sticks her punani in front of it. It's either eat up or shut up.

I have known Marvin for over a year, and now he's expressing his interest in me when I've decided to move away from Houston. We could have been getting it on a long time ago. Just the thought of Marvin with his fine ass is making me wet between the legs. I was jerked out of my daydreaming by Theresa's voice, "Oleather, what's wrong with you, girl. You are just sitting there like you are in a daze. Are you still going to lunch with me?"

"Yeah, girl, it's still on."

"Where is your mind anyway?"

"On my man back in Houston, Heartland."

"Houston!" Theresa sounded like she could not believe her ears. "Are you planning on getting involved in a long-distance relationship? Girl, girl, girl, let's get the hell out of this office so that I can give you the 411 on what you are about to get yourself into. Whose driving, you or me? On second thought, I'll drive because you seem to be a bit too out of focus to be doing any driving right now, and I am too young to...."

"Girl, you are crazy, slow down and let's go."

"Welcome to Burger King. May I help you?" The white lady's voice came through the speaker at the order board. Theresa ordered a fish combo meal, and I ordered the same. The weather was lovely, so we decided to eat outside. Theresa looked at me with curiosity written all over her face.

"How long have you been dating this man, Oleather?" she inquired,

"Well, it's not like that. We have known each other for over a year but never really expressed our private attraction to each other until I was leaving Houston."

Theresa raised an eyebrow, "so, my dear, it's safe to say you haven't screwed him yet. What do you honestly want from him, Oleather? How are you sure he's what you want?"

I hesitated in thought, "I have watched this man for several months, and I like what I see. When he told me he was interested, I reciprocated. That's all! I figured I'd give it a try."

"Girl, he must be a sexy motherfucker if you are saving him the kitty kat." We both laughed at Theresa's forward comment.

"Girl, you are crazy," I told Theresa. "A relationship is based or should be based, on more than just sex. I love sex, but I need more than sex; besides, if I don't try, I'll never know what could come out of this."

Theresa looked at me a sighed, "You're right, but I have to tell you, that long-distance thing is more than a mere challenge; it can become an emotional nightmare. I've been there, and I've done that. Needless to say, it didn't work."

"Theresa, you have to think out of the box and not be so narrow-minded. This could be the man I end up marrying," I told Theresa, who was now looking at me and rolling her eyes.

"What if he never proposes?"

"Well," I said, "life will go on as it usually does."

"Girlfriend," Theresa said, "I am just worried about your heart. I don't want to see you hurt and heartbroken."

"Well, it comes with the territory of being a grown-up. I think I can handle the pain and am looking forward to the pleasure."

"I sure do hope there is more pleasure than pain," Theresa mused, "and that you are not disappointed." We both laughed.

"Seriously though," Theresa said, "I'll be there for you whenever you need me. I'll share my shoulders with you so you can cry on them if you need to. And, if things go according to your desires, girl, I'll be the happiest for you too."

"Thanks, girl," I said, "just be my friend, OK?" I know Theresa was apprehensive about me because, "based on statistics," according to her, long-distance relationships rarely come to anything good. She said it definitely does not turn her on.

"Could be *your* problem," she said. "You know, why can't it be my happiness instead of my problem?" I lashed back defensively.

"Theresa, you need to take more chances. Just because you had a failed long-distance relationship does not mean you should predict doom for anyone else's relationship."

"You know Oleather; I just don't have faith in a man who lives out of town." To get the conversation wrapped up, I told Theresa we should be heading back to the office.

"Oleather, come on now, we still have a few more minutes. I know you are trying to get me to shut the hell up, but I am not through with you."

"Theresa, forget it. I know you mean well, and you are my best friend but let me have my own experiences, OK?"

"I don't think I can, Oleather, but I love you and will respect your wishes."

Truly Adore You

It's been a long day on the job. I could use a glass of wine and a little Oleather to go with dinner tonight. I figured since I couldn't have one, I'd have the other. I stopped at a local liquor store and noticed quite a few patrons who maybe felt partially the way I did today.

"Good evening, sir, welcome to Liquor Plus." It was a man of Middle Eastern descent behind the counter with an ear-to-ear grin on his face.

"Good evening to you, sir," I said, "I'd like to have a bottle of Kendall Jackson's Chardonnay, please."

"Will there be anything else?"

I thought for a second and said, "I'm afraid that'll be all, thank you." We wished each other good evenings, and I left.

Trying to determine what I wanted for dinner was more difficult than I had imagined. I finally decided on soul food. I got take-out from the "It's All Good" soul food restaurant. It was a good ten-minute drive from the house, but I figured it was worth it.

"Hello Marvin, what'll it be today?" Mary, the lead attendant, was a very bubbly, overweight woman with beady eyes and a sweet demeanor.

"Hi Mary, everything looks so good. I think I'll have some gravy and rice, macaroni and cheese, some collard greens, and two pieces of fried chicken – white meat."

"You gon eat here, Marvin?"

"Naw, I'll take it to go. Thanks!" I handed her a $10.00 bill and told her to keep the change.

She smiled and blew me a kiss. "Thanks, baby," she said, and I left.

On my way home, listening to Nelly's and P. Diddy's "Tailfeather," I couldn't wait to go home and relax in the comfort of my walls. I wondered what Oleather was doing. Once I pulled up and got into the apartment, I couldn't wait to call Oleather to remind her she was my lady now.

The phone rang for a while then… "You have reached Oleather at 843-777-9311. Sorry I am not here to take your call.…"

"Damn," I said out loud. I wanted to hear Oleather's voice. "What's up, Oleather?" I said into the receiver; I was just sitting here in my living room listening to some Miles Davis and thinking about you. Give me a call when you get in, okay baby, I'd love to talk with you." I hung up and decided to call her back in an hour or so.

I unpacked my dinner and sprawled in front of the tube. As I listened to Miles wash away the day's waves, I turned the TV down low so that I could have the best of both worlds. I drifted away in thought, wishing I had the opportunity to attend one of Miles' concerts before he died. He was indeed a gifted musician and a helluva black man. One of my favorite albums by Miles is "The

Birth of the Cool," featuring Miles live, John Coltrane, Bill Evans, and Cannon Bill. I can't think of the others right now, but I am sure enjoying the sounds.

The telephone rang, and I stopped my swaying. With a piece of chicken in one hand, I reached for the telephone with the other.

"Hello," "Hi Marvin, it's Oleather."

"Hi sweetie, how are you?"

"I'm alright," Oleather said. "Just getting off work. I got your message and decided to return your call. I could not wait to hear your voice either."

I smiled, feeling reassured of my position in Oleather's life. "Are you sure, Oleather, about our relationship?"

"I am as serious as a heart attack. Marvin."

"That's serious, baby?"

Oleather answered, "Yes, that's serious, and would you please not call me baby? Call me anything else. Men tend to use that word too loosely. I don't want you to get into that habit."

I was getting used to Oleather's bluntness and her natural way of not holding back her feelings. "I respect that. Consider it done."

Oleather confided in me that her girlfriend Theresa did not think our relationship would last because of the "long-distance" thing. "Oleather, I am sure we will hear from many people about the pros and cons of our long-distance relationship. What is more important is how we feel about it. Are you comfortable with your decision?"

"Yes," she said.

"That's all that matters then," I assured her. I am falling in love with you, Oleather. I am not ashamed to tell you that."

"I love you too, Marvin, and it feels damn good."

Oleather and I mutually agreed that we would do everything in our power to base our newly found happiness on faith and trust. We committed that nothing will keep us apart except time and space. When I think of Oleather, I am so happy to know that a woman is reserving her love for me.

"Marvin," Oleather broke the seconds of silence, "Are you seeing or sleeping with anyone else?"

"No, Oleather, I am not."

"I believe you." I could almost hear the smile in her voice as she was reassured that she was the one and only in my life.

"Your turn," I said, "how about you, do you have any desires for another man?"

"Sure don't. You're it for me, Marvin." She was serious. "Marvin, I know when we see each other this time around, sparks will fly like a 4th of July night in downtown Houston.

"We'll see to that for sure," Marvin said, chuckling, "well, I better not tie up your phone line any longer. I'll let you go do what you do when you get off work, and I'll call you over the weekend, okay?"

"Okay, Marvin. Call me on Saturday around 8:00 pm."

"I love you, Oleather. Goodnight and sweet dreams."

"Goodnight, Marvin. I love you too."

I Think I Found My Soulmate

Marvin was in the middle of a dream... actually, it was more of a nightmare when the phone rang. Jumping out of his sleep, heart racing, Marvin managed a groggy "Hello."

"Hi there sexy, did I wake you?"

"Hi, baby.... I mean, sweetheart," Marvin said, remembering Oleather's dislike for the misuse of the word "baby," "you could not have called at a better time; it's soooo good to hear your voice. Apart from having a bad dream, I forgot to set my alarm.

"Great, I've done my good deed for the day then," Oleather said.

"I owe you one."

"Don't worry, I'll cash in later," she said, chuckling.

"So, tell me, honey, how's the new job coming along?"

"It's actually okay. My first day was not too bad. I got hands-on experience yesterday when I saw a parolee get sent back to jail for a violation he committed."

"I'm sure this is just the beginning of such an experience Mr. Parole Officer. It comes with the territory, you know."

"Alright, smarty-pants, watch your mouth, or I'll have to sentence you to a spanking for messing with your boyfriend's mind so early in the morning."

"Don't tempt me. Anyway, I hope you have a wonderful day. I just wanted to hear your voice, wish you a good day, and tell you congratulations again on your new job. As always, please be careful."

"I will. Thanks, sweetie. Have a good day yourself, and I'll talk with you later."

Marvin rushed to the shower; nothing like a hot shower to get the day off to a great start. He had just spoken to the lady of his dreams, and there was nothing anyone could do or say at that point to spoil his day; he was on cloud nine. Marvin draped a huge towel around his muscular body and instinctively reached for his remote control. "Where the hell did I put the remote to the damn TV?" Marvin drank so much wine the night before he hadn't a clue as to where his remote was. He walked over to the television set and manually turned it on, flipping to the channel to his most-watched morning show—the Today Show hosted by Katie and Bryan. Keeping in tune with current events was a definite must as far as Marvin was concerned. He watched as discussions ensued about the Kosovo crisis as he ate his usual breakfast consisting of grain cereal and milk, a cup of peppermint tea, and an apple. Marvin's thoughts circled the injustices in the world. He thought about how the media treated people of color. A few years ago, when killing was rampant in Rwanda, no one raised hell about it; now, it's white on white crime, and the entire world is aware. As far as Marvin was concerned, the white man would never be fair when it came to people of color. He decided, since he could not single-handedly change the world, he'd better get dressed and get into the office.

"Good morning Mr. Kenyatta." It was Ms. Jones's perky voice greeting him as he entered the office.

"Good morning, Ms. Jones; how are you today? Would you please buzz me in?"

"Not a problem. Remind me today to get you a key to the office."

"I'll do that." Marvin walked down the hall and almost bumped into Ms. Rodriquez.

"Good morning, Mr. Kenyatta; I'm sorry; I almost knocked you over. I was expecting an important call and was rushing to my office before I missed it."

"Not a problem at all." As Ms. Rodriquez continued walking, she asked Marvin to come by her office when he got a chance. She wanted to show him something on the computer.

"I'll get settled in, and I'll call you before coming over."

"Sounds great! See you in a little bit."

Upon walking into his office, Marvin was reminded of his incomplete benefits package. He decided to complete it after he visited with Ms. Rodriquez. After checking in with Ms. Rodriquez, Marvin went over to her office.

"Come on in, Mr. Kenyatta. Would you like a cup of coffee before we get started?"

"Oh, no, thank you. I don't drink coffee; I am more into tea."

"Not a problem; I'll get you a cup of herbal tea."

"Thank you; I do appreciate that." Ms. Rodriquez came back with two cups. One with a tea bag string hanging over the side, and the other was her coffee. "Mr. Edmond wanted me to show you around our internal system on the computer. It's not very difficult maneuvering around it. We use the intranet quite a bit for locating frequently used forms and for getting answers to FAQs. Feel free to stop me at any time." Marvin soon learned the system was very user-friendly and took to it almost immediately.

The halls of the office and the people that worked there were becoming very familiar now. Marvin was beginning to feel a lot more comfortable with his surroundings. Ms. Rodriquez took Marvin to visit the Communications department per Mr. Edmond's request. As they walked down the hall, Marvin's mind went to the stack of paperwork on his desk that needed to be completed. He hoped that what Ms. Rodriquez had to show him would not take up too much time. Marvin streamlined everything he did to utilize his time best. You could say he was organized to the fault.

"Good morning Ms. Jackson. How is your day going so far?"

"So far, I have no complaints. Thank you! Good morning Mr. Uh...."

"Ms. Jackson, this is Marvin Kenyatta. Mr. Kenyatta is our newest Parole Officer."

"Hello Ms. Jackson, it's very nice to meet you."

"My pleasure. The name Kenyatta is different. Is it Indian?"

"No, ma'am, its actual origination is Africa."

"Call me Marie. Please have a seat."

"Now that you and Marie have met, Marie heads up the Communications department. She keeps us informed of any news, changes, etc., as it relates to the prisons and parolees here in Heartland. Marie gets articles daily, which have anything to do with the penal system with updates and things of such. You will notice copied articles in your mailbox or inbox daily. It is recommended you read the information. This helps officers get a better understanding about the seriousness of our jobs."

"Speaking of articles and jobs, here's an article I just got off the fax machine. If you don't mind, make a copy for your reading pleasure and return it to me please once you're done."

"Great! Thanks, Marie. I'll have it on your desk in a little bit."

Ms. Rodriquez decided to take Marvin to the lab. "You know Marvin; you seem to be blending in very well. Don't let the parolees drive you crazy. They can do that, you know."

"Oh, I think I'm ready," Marvin said. Then, with a hint of sarcasm, he added, "One of the reasons I accepted the position."

"You do look like you are a very strong man. I know everything's going to be just fine." "Thank you. I do appreciate that."

"Hello, Mr. Pete. Good morning!"

"Marnin' Miz Rodriquez," came the reply from Gerald Pete. Mr. Pete was an older black man who talked with an African accent. His words sounded as though they were being cut short, but yet they weren't. His gray hair and mustache brought back beautiful memories of Marvin's grandfather. His smile lit up the room, and Marvin knew he would love working with this man.

"How can I be of help to you today?"

"Mr. Pete, this is Marvin Kenyatta. Marvin is our newest Parole Officer."

"Very nice to meet ya, Mauvin...I hope ya doan mine me callin' ya Mauvin."

"Please, Mr. Pete, call me Marvin. I'd like that."

"Welcome aboard!" he said, giving my right hand a firm shake.

"Thank you, sir, and I am looking forward to working with you."

Mr. Pete continued, "This is called de piss lab." I smiled, and Mr. Pete laughed heartily, "Just kiddin' there fella, eet ees called de Urinalysis lab. Parolees have to submit de urine samples in dese cups, and we test eet in de machine for drugs. Remember, not to let de clients urinate in dis office." He laughed again and continued, "de restroom ees next door. Don't make de mistake of going into de ladies' restroom. Male parolees go weet male officers, and de female parolees go weet de female officers."

At this point, we were all laughing. "You are too crazy, Mr. Pete," Ms. Rodriquez said, still laughing. "Let's move on, Marvin, so that Mr. Pete can get back to what he was doing. He's given you the first serious lesson for the day."

Marvin and Ms. Rodriquez walked back to her office. "Well, Marvin, in about a week or so, you should receive a user I.D. and password to enter the computer. That process takes a little longer than you would expect."

Marvin was standing over Ms. Rodriquez' shoulders, paying keen attention to what she was doing on the computer. "Every piece of information regarding your clients must be entered into the computer. There is also lots of paperwork involved. I would advise you to get into the habit of entering all your clients' information as soon as possible instead of letting them pile up. This will save you from a headache or buttache one day."

"I'll remember that. Thanks."

"I will be the one responsible for your training until you can handle it on your own, so don't be hesitate to ask any question you may have."

Ring, ring, ring...Ms. Rodriquez pressed the speaker button on her phone and answered with a loud "hello...Mr. Spencer Hayes? Great! Thank you, Ms. Jones." Upon disconnecting the call, Ms. Rodriquez explained she had a client in the lobby and asked Marvin to escort him to her office. By this time, Marvin was getting the hang of his job. "Not a problem; I'll be right back."

"Thank you, Marvin. Make sure he walks in front of you. Always have the parolees walk ahead of you at all times; it's a safety precaution."

"Will do."

"Mr. Spencer Hayes," Marvin said out loud with an air of authority.

"Here," came the voice in the lobby waiting area.

"Mr. Hayes, please come with me; Ms. Rodriquez is waiting." Marvin, remembering what Ms. Rodriquez had told him, walked behind Mr. Hayes. Mr. Hayes looked like he would not hurt a fly, let alone go to prison.

"Good morning Mr. Hayes," said Ms. Rodriquez "how are you doing today?"

"Fine, Ms. Rodriquez."

"Have you stayed out of trouble since I saw you last?"

"Yes, ma'am."

"How about your employment? Are you still working at Burger King?"

"Yes, ma'am, still flipping those burgers every day."

"Good. Don't work yourself too hard."

"I'll try not to."

"Mr. Hayes, this is Marvin Kenyatta, one of our new Parole Officers. I am training Mr. Kenyatta, and he will be sitting in on today's meeting." Ms. Rodriquez opened Mr. Hayes' yellow folder and thumbed through some pages. She made some notes and continued with her questioning. "So, Mr. Hayes, tell me, how are things really going with you?"

"Not too bad, Ms. Rodriquez. Some of my old drug buddies have been callin' me up to hang out. I always have a good excuse not to go, though. You know Ms. Rodriquez, I been tryin' to clean up my life. I did mess my life up once, and I refuse to do it twice. Ten years in prison was enough for me."

"That's great news! How is your family?"

"My parents are doin' fine. The both of them are so proud of me for makin' the right choice and doin' the right thing...you know, workin' and not hangin' out in the streets."

"Have you given any thought to our last conversation, the one about getting back into school and taking up a trade or something you like?"

"Yes, ma'am, but I have never been very good with books."

"Maybe, Mr. Hayes, you are good with your hands."

"Well, the manager at Burger King said I make very good hamburgers."

"Maybe, you can become a cook."

"Never thought of it. I did use to help the cooks when I was in prison."

"Great then, I'll make some phone calls to some vocational schools to get more direction; then we'll go from there. What do you think?"

"That will be good." Mr. Hayes seemed very sincere and enthusiastic about making his life better. "Do you have your fees for today, Mr. Hayes?"

"Yes, ma'am, I have a money order." He handed the money order to Ms. Rodriquez.

"Okay, Mr. Hayes, it was nice seeing you again and to hear that things are going well. Have a nice day."

"Thank you, Ms. Rodriquez. You have a nice day too. Very nice meeting you, Mr. Kenyatta; did I say it right?"

"Perfect," Marvin said, and he escorted Mr. Hayes to the exit.

"Wait!" Ms. Rodriquez said, "I need you to leave a urine sample, Mr. Hayes. You are familiar with the procedure; here's your cup. Mr. Kenyatta, would you mind taking Mr. Hayes to the restroom?"

"Glad to."

"Whew, I was holding my pee for thirty minutes. Glad to go."

"Get out of here," laughed Ms. Rodriquez.

After Mr. Hayes was through using the restroom, he blurted out, "Oooooh, that felt soooo good, man. Have you ever wanted to pee so badly and had to hold it? Then when it comes out, it feels so good, like a load taken off you."

"I know the feeling." Mr. Hayes placed the cup with urine in the cooler, washed his hands, and walked back to the office with Marvin. Ms. Rodriquez completed her paperwork, and Marvin escorted Mr. Hayes to the exit.

"Marvin, I do hope you picked up some pointers from my interview."

"I did."

"Just keep in mind, these parolees are human beings. Don't try to make them feel less than that. I say this to you because Parole Officers tend to abuse their authority and be very mean to the parolees. You can accomplish a lot more with sugar than vinegar if you know what I mean."

"Yes, ma'am, I understand."

"On the other hand, though, remember, they are parolees, and you always need to be in control."

"I'm learning, Ms. Rodriquez; I'm learning."

"You will be a great Parole Officer Marvin. I just know you will."

I'm On Your Side

Theresa was just stepping out of the shower when she heard a knock on the door. "Shit," Theresa said out loud. "Who the hell can be stopping by so late and have the nerve to not call before coming over." Then she remembered she had asked Frank to stop by to talk before he went to work. "Frank?"

"It's me, baby. Open up." "How are you doing, baby?" Frank was not exactly what you would call cute, more of a playboy type, fine as hell, always dressed to the nines, and smelled good too.

"I'm fine."

"You sounded like this was important on the phone. Can I get a kiss?"

"Is that all you want?"

"Well, since you asked, no – what I want is what's between yo legs." This was the kind of stuff that turned Theresa on about Frank, the kind of thing she liked about her thug lover. She loved to play along with his antics.

"You've been a bad boy Frankie; you need to be punished. I am not giving you any kisses. You are hereby sentenced to licking my pussy until I cum. Then, when I do, I may just let you have your way with me. Frank could feel the hardness in his pants increase with every ounce of anticipation how he longed to feel Theresa's warmness, the warmness that always welcomed him.

"Not out here, Let' go to the room."

"I'll get pillows; it's better on the floor." "Lick me, Frankie, taste my sweet honey...Ummm" Frank satisfied Theresa's desires. As they lay on the floor exhausted, Theresa propped her head in the palm of her hands and leaned over to Frank. "Frank, would you mind giving me a massage?"

"Not at all baby, go to the bathroom and bring the massage oil." Theresa came back with the oil and handed it to Frank. Frank seemed a little hesitant.

"What's up, baby? You are acting like you don't know what to do anymore. Pour it on my back and rub it in." Frank rubbed the oil on Theresa's back.

"That's right, harder, baby. Let me feel your strength."

"Enough with the suspense," Frank blurted, "you got me real curious wondering what's going on with you."

"Okay, Frank, this is the deal; my girlfriend Oleather just moved back to town about a month ago. She doesn't have a man in town, and she is moving into her new home this coming Saturday. Can you and your cousin Joe come by and help us move?"

"That's what was so important? That's what you had to tell me and couldn't do it on the phone?"

"Frank, yes, it is important to me, and I have to confess, I was kinda' feigning you."

"Is your girlfriend gonna have some food and drinks up in the house?"

"Yes, Frank, I told her what you liked, and she said not to worry."

"Cool, what time Saturday morning, and what's the address?" Theresa told Frank to be there about 9:30 a.m. and reiterated for him to bring Joe.

"My girlfriend been alone for such a long time; I know she could use a nice hard dick."

"Now, how do you know that?"

"She's woman, ain't she? And I am a woman, aren't I? We just know these things."

"You think maybe your girl's gonna take to Joe?"

"Hmmm, I like the thought of that. You never know. On second thought, that will have to be her decision all the way. I am not even going there." All this freak talk was making Theresa hot once again. Frank showered her body with kisses while they fell into an ocean of passion and satisfaction. Frank, exhausted, took a quick shower, dressed, and left for work. Theresa felt relaxed and contented. She fell into a deep sleep consumed by dreams of Frank and her traveling to different places and experiencing passion and climaxes in the most unmentionable of places.

My Prayers Are With You

The telephone was ringing. "Hello"

"Hi Marvin, it's me, Oleather. How are you, honey?"

"Hi sweetheart, I was just thinking about you. I'm doing a'ight."

"Great minds think alike, they say. I guess I just beat you to the punch."

"So, what's been going on, sweetie."

"I am planning my move into my new house on Saturday."

"I sure do wish I was there to help you get moved and settled in. I guess congratulations are in order. You're now officially a permanent resident of Charleston, South Carolina."

"How many bedrooms?" "Four, and the master have your name above the door."

"Ummm, I think I like the sound of that. What are you doing right now anyway?"

"Walking into the bedroom."

"What are you wearing?" Marvin's voice was low and seductive.

"I'd get naked if you want me to.... Marvin, are you initiating a phone sex session with me?"

"Maybe, you game?"

"Just imagine Marvin, you walk into my bedroom, and I am wearing a red G-string and a very skimpy top that matches. I am on my King-sized bed with lightly scented candles, flames dancing romantically, making strange shadows on the wall. Imagine the color of my skin against the dim flickering lights; I am longing for you, and you can see it in my eyes, the windows to my soul...."

"Oleather, I am so with you right now. I...I can imagine you, sweetie. I can't wait to hold you, Oleather..., to be with you, to kiss you and love you."

"Did you ever finalize your travel date?"

"Oh, yes, I sure did. I was going to give you a call with the complete info. You have a pen handy?" Marvin gave Oleather a date of July 9th, two weeks away. July 9th was a Friday.

"I am so ready for you to come, Marvin. I have been on drought, and I need some watering," Marvin laughed at Oleather's choice of words.

"Marvin, when you get here, be prepared for the pampering of your life. I am going to cook for you, give you a world-class 'Oleather massage,' honey, and I am going to give you such good love, you'll be addicted."

"Girl, don't be talking like that. You are going to make a brother pass out." Oleather laughed out loud, and it felt so good. It was so genuine. Oleather felt a rare closeness to Marvin.

"Oleather, you are making my dick hard, girl."

Had I Only Known

"Down, boy, two weeks will be here before you know it. Not to worry, I'll turn you into a naughty boy before the weekend is over."

"I love you, Oleather. I'll just take a cold shower and look forward to seeing you on the 9th.

"I love you too, Marvin. Sweet dreams."

When You Think of Me

The phone rang six times before Oleather picked up. She answered in a tired-sounding voice. "Girl, you better wake your ass up. Do you remember what day it is? Let me remind you. It's Saturday, girl; you are moving...Hello, are you with me? The boys and I are on our way to take the shit out of storage."

"Shit, ok, ok, I'm up. I'll meet you guys at the U-Haul Storage yard at 3325 King Street in 20 minutes."

"Did you get the stuff for the boys? You know they are going to be looking forward to grub and drinks when they are done."

"Girl, that's been taken care of. Theresa, I am so grateful to you for helping me out like this. What's a sister to do without a good friend like you?"

"Yeah, you know I love your ass. Just get over here."

"Okay, I'll see ya in 20 minutes." Click.

"Is your girl ready or what?"

"She's ready. We could go pick up Joe; we're meeting her in twenty minutes on King Street."

"Cool!" Frank gave Theresa a friendly pat on her butt.

Joe was looking pretty sexy in his faded and torn jeans and a Sean Jean tee shirt. "Wazzup ya'll?" Joe greeted Theresa and Frank.

"Everything's cool. Ready for work?"

"I guess so, Terri," Joe always called Theresa 'Terri'.

"Is this gonna be a blind date or what?"

"Boy, who said anything about a blind date? This is more of a working party."

"Well, what's the possibility of me getting a little ass once we're done?"

"A little forward, aren't we?" Theresa said sarcastically.

"I guess that'll be up to you and fate now, won't it?"

"Aww, Terri, why you always gots to shoot a brother down."

"No, Joe, for real, play your cards right. You never know...."

"What does she look like, Frankie?"

"I don't know, man; you gotta get your information from Theresa."

"Terri?"

"She's fine. As a matter of fact, she's a fox with a nice ass."

"You mean like a basketball?"

"I don't' know bout all that. You'll see soon enough. No promises from me, though."

"Aight' you guys, let's get to steppin," Frank said.

Oleather's red convertible was already parked at the Storage when Theresa and the guys got there. Oleather was in the back seat with the door open; she was looking for something. When Frank blew his horn, Oleather jumped. At that point, they were all laughing. "Oleather, this is my boyfriend Frank and his cousin Joe."

"Hey guys, it's very nice to meet you. I just want to let you know I appreciate you coming out here on a Saturday morning to help me out."

Frank and Joe took turns shaking Oleather's hand. "Nice to meet you, finally, Oleather. I have heard so much about you; it's like I've known you forever." Oleather laughed.

"I've heard a lot about you too, Oleather," Joe said, "and so far, Theresa is right on the money."

"Thanks, I think," Oleather said, giving Theresa a look that said 'I'm gonna get you later for this.'

"Follow me, guys; my unit is in the back." They got to the unit and started loading its contents into the truck Oleather had rented for the day. Once Oleather opened the door to her unit, Theresa could not help herself.

"Girl, you sure do have a shit load of stuff in here."

"I knew you would be the first to comment," Oleather said, and Theresa rolled her eyes. There was furniture and boxes upon boxes of stuff. Frank and Joe figured they should be able to make two trips to complete the move.

"Who's driving the U-Haul?" Oleather inquired.

"I will," said Joe, "providing you'll accompany me."

"I don't see why not," Oleather chirped.

"Great, let's do this." Joe took charge by getting the keys and backing up the truck. Oleather was impressed by his aggressiveness. The girls did their share of work, with Theresa constantly complaining of how heavy the boxes were, but Frank and Joe were like human machines. Oleather admired the pair. The music from the truck was blasting. It made the packing a little easier and made the atmosphere more relaxing.

Finally, they had completed the first set of packing and were turning off King Street. Oleather and Joe made small talk, and Oleather decided Joe was not a bad person. A little bold but nothing she could not handle. They pulled up in front of Oleather's new house. Everyone was impressed with Oleather's four-bedroom home, three baths (two upstairs and one on the first floor), and spacious living room. While Joe was thinking about claiming one of the rooms, particularly the one Oleather will be adorning herself in each night, Theresa burst out, "Girlfriend, what are you supposed to do with such a big house?"

"Well, I intend to live like a queen. Girl, I work my ass off so, I deserve this."

"I hear you," Frank said.

"Well, your royal highness, where are your servants' food and drink?"

"Sure, drinks are in the refrigerator, and the food will be delivered hot from Kroger's deli at 12:30. So, since it's only 11:00, I guess...."

"Actually, Oleather, I am not quite yet hungry, but I sure can use a beer."

"Me too," Joe added. The guys got their drinks and started to unload the truck.

"Okay, your highness, your humble slave girl will get back to work right away, ma'am," Theresa said.

"Girl, shut up! You are too much." Oleather told Theresa playfully. "Just bring your royal ass with me to complete this here work. You know where everything goes, so guide me." They had four more boxes to unload when the Kroger Deli truck pulled up. A tall young white man came to the door. He was wearing a light blue shirt and dark blue pants with a Kroger badge pinned to the top left of his shirt.

"Hello," he said, "I am looking for a Oleather Ellis?"

"I'm Oleather. Hi, how are you?"

"Where would you like me to put your delivery, ma'am?" he asked, his eyes peering at the boxes in the house.

"Here's fine," Oleather said, pointing to a dining table that was positioned in the foyer.

"Please excuse the mess; as you can see, I'm just moving in."

"No problem. Thanks for calling Kroger to assist." Oleather paid the young man, and he left. At this time, everyone was hungry.

"Alright, you guys, let's eat, drink, and be merry for tomorrow, we will be too tired," Theresa said, laughing.

"Don't let me have to spank you," Frank said, teasing Theresa. It was the perfect time to take a break and eat. The guys unloaded the four boxes, washed their hands, and they ate together over funny conversations.

Frank and Theresa disappeared, and Oleather and Joe continued their chatting. "I wonder where those two disappeared to? They've been gone for 10 minutes now."

"I am not sure," Joe said, "but I don't mind disappearing with you, Oleather."

"Okay, you have got me bent, Joe. I have a man that's coming into town in two weeks. That's number one. Number two, you barely met me, and I sure as hell don't know you. So, for you to be so forward, I consider it disrespect."

"Girl, I been watching your fine ass while you were moving boxes, and man, it turned me the shit on."

"Okay, you have had one too many beers. There is nothing wrong with watching and seeing; just don't get the wrong impression."

"How about me just touching your ass? Or you rub my dick? Geez, girl, you makin' a nigga' horny as hell. Come on, don't think about it; let's do the nasty."

"Go fuck yourself, Joe. Get the hell out of my house." Joe was still standing there with a glazed look over his face, his pants unbuttoned and his manhood visible and erect. "My man is a Parole Officer, and I will call him in an instant if you don't get moving."

"Man, you don't got to be like that."

"GET OUT" Oleather screamed as she ran around the kitchen, trying frantically to escape Joe's apparent drunkenness. At this point, Joe was having lots of fun. Frank and Theresa came running out to see what the commotion was. Frank was buttoning his shirt, and Theresa was fully dressed.

"What the hell is going on here?" Theresa shouted.

"Get this stupid ass motherfucker out of my house right now, or else; I am calling the police," Oleather shouted hysterically. "He's trying to rape me."

"Shit, I thought you said this bitch was gonna gimme some Terri; what's up with that, huh?"

"Joe, you trippin' like a motherfucker, get the hell out of Oleather's house. You and I had no such discussion. Get OUT!" "Oleather, I am so sorry about this shit. If I had known this ass would not be able to hold a few beers and control that stupid ass libido of his, I would have never encouraged him to come over. I'll make sure he leaves, and you won't cross paths again, at least not if I have anything to do with it. Joe, I'll talk with you later. You've done enough damage, man. Go home. Shooting your damn mouth off like a fucking rifle."

"Aight' I'm leaving. Sorry, Oleather." Joe looked ashamed as he left. Oleather was crying at this point, and Theresa was consoling her.

"Theresa, what the hell did you tell Joe about me for him to get the impression that I am just a fuck away?"

"Oleather, I swear to God, I did not tell Joe anything of the sort, much less give him the impression that you were a clothes clip."

"It's okay, you guys. Thanks so much for your help, but I do need some time to me. I'll call movers; I'm sure it won't be a problem."

"Oleather, I am sorry, let me stay...."

"Theresa, it's okay. Frank, nothing against you; I just need to be alone with my thoughts right now. You understand, don't you?"

"I understand, Oleather. Look, I am sorry. It was very nice meeting you, and I hope we can get together under better circumstances."

"It was nice meeting you too. I'll see you guys later. Theresa, I'll call you. In the meantime, I had better get to making some phone calls to complete this move."

"Bye, Oleather."

Theresa knew she was in trouble with Oleather and decided to 'let sleeping dogs lie.' They left. Luckily for Oleather, she had left her car in the U-Haul parking lot, so she returned the U-Haul and drove her car back home. Fortunately, Oleather's first phone call got her a mover who was available to come by in "one hour and a half." At the end of it all, Oleather was exhausted. She decided to work overtime in getting the house together before her visit from Marvin. She took a long hot bath. Oleather had to hunt through boxes to retrieve a comforter that would suffice for the night. She felt as though she had run 10 miles. She was physically and mentally drained, which is why when she placed her head on the pillow, she did not awake until the alarm sounded at 7:00 a.m. on Sunday. Oleather planned on taking a couple of sick days – Monday and Tuesday to complete her project at home.

Oh! How I Love You

Oleather ran to pick up the phone that had just started ringing.

"Hi Oleather, it's Marvin, sweetie. How are things going?"

"It's fine. Oh, Marvin, I can't believe the time has come for you to be here. I am so excited, honey. Where are you?"

"Well, I called to tell you that I am unable to make the trip. You see, I met this girl, and she tied me up so...."

"Would you quit playing around, silly?"

"You know me too well; can't even lie with a straight face. I am now leaving work, and I'm on my way to the airport. Thank God it's Friday. You haven't misplaced my flight information, have you?"

"Of course not; I have been thinking about you so much this week; I think I may have it memorized." They both laughed.

"Great, I will see you at the airport."

"Oh no, honey, I am taking a cab to your house. I think you forget your promise to me." "Promise, what promise are you talking about?"

"Remember? You will be opening the door in your red, silk nightgown, 4-inch pumps, and sipping on a glass of wine. The room will be candlelit, and the incense will be burning...."

"Oh, you are right. Honey, I am so ready to see you...."

"Don't worry; it'll all be in good time. Stick to our plans."

"I know, sweetie, but the more I think of it, the more I think it's a good idea for me to meet you. You'll save a hell of a lot of money. Besides, when we get home, we can prepare our Boudoir just the way we envisioned. We could take a nice hot bath together, and the rest will be sheer ecstasy."

"You are so convincing. Okay, I give up. I'll be the guy in the baggy jeans and the tan-colored Tommy Hilfiger tee."

"And I'll be the cute girl with the white blouse, red shorts, and no underwear."

"Funny."

"Marvin, I hope to have you have been drinking a lot of ginseng tea?"

"Yes; why?"

"Well, you'll need it. You will need the strength in all the right places."

"Girl, all that talk, I hope you can handle what I am bringing to the table."

"Oooh, I am so scared. Bring it on. All you need to do is stay hard; I can handle the rest."

"Alright, big talker, I'll get the proof in a few hours." "A few hours, I like the sound of that."

"See you in a few then." Oleather hung up the phone and felt like a kid about to be showered with presents.

At 10:05 p.m., Marvin's flight landed. "Flight 427 from Houston has arrived. Passengers will be unloading in just a few minutes...." The lady's voice on the loudspeaker was clear and crisp. Oleather felt her heart racing with anticipation. Marvin, on the other hand, was very anxious. His mind immediately drifted to Oleather's outfit. Was she wearing the white blouse and red shorts like she said? Was she wearing no underwear? The mere thought gave him an instant hard-on.

"Shit, control yourself, Marvin; this could be embarrassing." Marvin did not realize he was thinking out loud.

"Excuse me, sir," the old lady sitting on his right said.

"Oh, sorry, ma'am, I was just thinking out a little too loud." If Marvin's skin color were lighter, the redness that overtook his handsome face would have been very noticeable. The lady gave Marvin a strange look and proceeded to retrieve her luggage from the overhead bin.

"Marvin," Oleather hugged Marvin so hard that Marvin joked.

"I can't breathe."

"Shut up, Marvin, you know you like it."

"God, it's so good to see you, sweetie. Let me prove it." Marvin pulled Oleather closer to him and kissed her passionately. It was as though there was no one else there. Marvin had his luggage on the plane, so there was no need to go to the baggage claim area.

Oleather pulled into the driveway, and Marvin was impressed. Once they got in, the air felt so good in the house, and it smelled good too. Marvin looked around and complimented Oleather on her choice. "You did great, honey. This is a gorgeous house. I can't imagine you in here, by yourself with all this room."

"It's okay. I like the idea. Make yourself comfortable, Marvin. I'll pour you a glass of something to take a load off. What would you prefer, wine or cognac?"

"Tough choice. Do you have any Jack Daniels?"

"Sure."

Oleather walked over to the bar and fixed two glasses, "turn on the CD player honey, play something nice... something romantic."

"How about some Marvin Gaye?"

"That's what I'm talking about." Oleather brought back the drinks, and Marvin's eyes were gleaming with excitement.

"You know, honey; ever since I got off the plane, I wanted to ask you something."

"And what would that something be?" Oleather had a hint of mischievousness in her eyes.

"Well, I wanted to know if you were not wearing any underwear."

"Okay, Mr. Kenyatta, why don't you see for yourself?"

Marvin moved closer to Oleather and started to unbutton her shorts. *God, I have been waiting for this moment for so long.* Marvin thought. Oleather eased herself in an upward motion giving Marvin all the leverage he needed to complete his task. To Marvin's delight, Oleather was indeed not wearing any panties.

"Like what you see, Marvin?" she asked seductively.

"Oh Oleather, you are beautiful and edible too." After Marvin had a full view of Oleather's beautiful curves, Oleather decided it was her turn. She slowly took off Marvin's T-Shirt.

"I really would like to see what I am getting to know," Oleather said as she unzipped Marvin's pants. As she took off his underwear, Oleather gasped with excitement. "Marrrrvin, wow, hold me, baby. I am ready for you like I have never been ready for anything or anyone before." Oleather welcomed Marvin's tongue as he pulled Oleather closer to him; Oleather felt as though she would melt.

"Like what you see?" Marvin asked.

"Yes, honey, I love what I see."

"Oh sweetheart, you taste delicious." They were completely naked at this point, and with Marvin Gaye crooning in the background, and the candles were flickering; Oleather and Marvin were in their own galaxy. They did not make it to the bedroom immediately but fell on the floor in passion. Oleather moved on top of Marvin and began kissing him passionately. Marvin moaned as Oleather moved her sexy hips over his erect manhood.

"I can't wait for us to become one, Marvin."

"Patience," Marvin whispered, I am not finished with you yet." Marvin rolled Oleather over and started kissing her lips, neck, breast; then he moved to Oleather's womanhood ever so softly. Oleather moaned and moved her hips to meet Marvin's hungry mouth.

"Please, Marvin, I need you right now, please," Oleather begged. "You sure do have a big dick Marvin, please don't hurt me."

"I'll be gentle with you, honey." At that point, Oleather took Marvin's hand and led him to the bathroom. Oleather's bathroom was beautiful. She turned on the shower, lit some scented candles then continued to kiss Marvin. It was like they could not get enough of each other. With the water glistening on their bodies, Marvin lifted Oleather. Instinctively, Oleather wrapped her legs around his waist and their tongues intertwined. Marvin was ready for Oleather as much as she was ready for him. As Marvin eased himself into Oleather's moistness, they both became weak with desire.

"All of you," Oleather gasped, "I want all of you inside of me."

"Oleather, you are so beautiful... you feel so good," Marvin whispered in her ear.

"Do you love me, Marvin?"

"Yes, Oleather, I love you. I love everything about you; the way you talk, walk, smile... hmm, I just love you."

"I love you too, Marvin. I love you so much." They both reached their point of satisfaction almost at the same time. Oleather's body convulsed, and Marvin was shaking uncontrollably. They finished showering and went to lie in bed. Marvin felt so wonderful. The feel of the red and black satin sheets, the music... nothing could be better. They lay in bed and talked for what seemed like hours.

"You know, honey, I have said this before but, I could really beat myself for not getting to know you on a more personal basis when you were in Houston."

"Well, you had the chance, but you did nothing."

"Okay, don't rub it in. When I first saw you in the office, I had many fantasies about you."

"Really, like what?"

"Girl, apart from you being fine as hell and owning the most beautiful behind, I wanted to be a part of your life and to get to know you better, but, as I told you before, I was worried about putting our jobs in jeopardy."

"Since all that's in the past, we'll just move on – better late than never, right?"

"Right."

"What was that you said about liking my behind?" Oleather turned on her stomach as if to let Marvin know it was all his.

"Umm, umm, umm, and this is all mine?" Marvin was like a kid in a candy store. He rubbed and kissed Oleather's luscious behind as though he was putting his mark on it. As Marvin's hand traveled down Oleather's legs and between her thighs, Oleather's moans became louder

"Ooooh, Marvin, you are making me wet all over again."

"Good, I like that." Marvin stroked Oleather's clitoris, and Oleather went wild as she begged for him to penetrate her. Upon Oleather's request, Marvin could not believe the feelings that rushed through his body. He continued to heave in and out of her moist canal until they both exploded with passion. They fell onto the satin sheets, exhausted and satisfied.

"Marvin, have I fulfilled your fantasy?"

"Yes, sweetheart, you did completely... in a mighty big way."

"Will I see you again after this weekend?"

"Oleather, if you are not sure, let me assure you that I am in this relationship for the long haul."

"I like to hear that because I feel the same way, Marvin. I feel the same way."

You Open My Heart

"Good morning, honey." Oleather looked at Marvin's handsome features for quite a while and decided to greet him when she saw him stir. She was elated by the way things went the night Marvin came into town.

"Hi, sweetheart," Marvin replied, rubbing his eyes and propping up on his elbow.

"Did I wake you?"

"Yes, but you are excused" Oleather gave Marvin a playful punch on the arm.

"How did you sleep?"

"Girl, would you believe it if I told you I slept like a baby?"

"Uh-huh, because I slept the same way."

"Sweetheart, last night was so wonderful. I assure you this will stay with me for a long time. I can't believe the weekend is just about over, and I will be leaving tomorrow."

"Hey, let's not dwell on it; let us make the best of it."

"How about some breakfast?"

"You are a sweetheart, but I am not hungry; I'll take some juice, please."

"My juice or orange juice?"

"Tough choice, but I think I'll settle for some OJ right now."

Oleather turned her lips down in a playful frown, "Your wish is my command, sir."

"I'm giving you time to build up your juices, and I like it when it flows."

"You have been hanging out with me for too long; my naughtiness is beginning to rub off."

Oleather and Marvin decided to do a little more sightseeing. They took pictures and even hung out at the zoo for a little while. Marvin especially liked the time they spent at the park. Oleather had packed a picnic basket, and they went to the park for some quiet time. It was 3:20 p.m. when Oleather looked at her watch. "Maybe, we should be heading back to the house, honey. We could make the best of things tonight before you leave.

"I trust your judgment honey, let's go. Besides, there are lots I want to leave you with to remember me." Marvin looked mysterious.

"I'm up for it... whatever it is," Oleather said, liking the idea.

On their way back to the house, Oleather called Theresa and invited her over to meet "my handsome man." Theresa, of course, would not have turned down the invitation even if there was a storm brewing. "I'll be there in a jiffy, girlfriend."

"See ya soon, bye."

Oleather and Marvin had been in the house for twenty minutes when there was a knock on the door. "That must be my crazy ass friend Theresa."

"I can't wait to meet her." Oleather did not mention the moving incident to Marvin. She decided that his first impression of Theresa must be pure.

"Hi there girlfriend, where's this lover man of yours?" Theresa shouted as though Oleather was a mile away.

"In the bedroom, where else?" Oleather kidded.

"Is he decent?"

"Marvin, honey Theresa is here." Marvin strutted out of the Master's room, looking as gorgeous as ever. He walked into the living room where Oleather and Theresa were standing.

"Marvin, this is Theresa, my crazy girlfriend."

"Hi Theresa, it's nice to meet you finally. I've heard lots about you." Marvin extended his hands to shake Theresa's but instead, Theresa gave Marvin an unexpected hug.

"If you are a friend of Oleather, you are automatically a friend of mine. It's very nice to meet you. I have heard a lot about you myself. I am happy you came to Charleston, and I know Oleather has shown you a royal time."

"I have to say, Theresa, this visit has been a great experience. Oleather is the best."

"Well, you hang in there, you have a few more hours, and I think there are lots more to come." Theresa winked at Marvin, and Oleather gave her a friendly push.

"What you got to eat up in here, gurl?"

"Since when you started asking for something to eat. Normally, you just take your crazy ass to the kitchen and get what you want."

"Well, your man is in the house so, I have to show my good side."

"Didn't know you had one," Oleather teased.

"Just don't change back to your old self when my man is gone."

"Girl, I ain't old."

"Not you, your habits."

"Now you are talking." Theresa turned to Marvin, "You know Marvin, I have known Oleather for over 35 years now. She ain't changed one bit, and I got worse." She laughed.

"Gone girl, go get your grub on in the kitchen like you're used to."

"Thanks, girl" Theresa went into the kitchen and put some Turkey sausages into the microwave.

"Why don't you bring Marvin to Jackie's party tonight?"

"Well, we kinda' want to spend the night alone, if you know what I mean."

"Go, gurl," Theresa shouted in her usual loud tone.

"It was very nice meeting you, Marvin. Sorry that I have to eat and run, but I think it'll be good to leave you two lovebirds alone. Marvin, I'll be praying for your safe return to Houston."

"Thanks, Theresa; it was nice meeting you."

"Bye, chill, chill, girlfriend."

"Chill, chill to you to Theresa, see you later."

Marvin and Oleather decided to stop by the Blockbuster around the corner to pick up some movies for the night they had planned.

"Ready when you are Oleather."

"I'm ready honey, let me just grab my pocketbook. I ordered some take-out, and it should be here in an hour. If we time ourselves right, we should be back home in about thirty minutes."

"Great, I am ready for some food."

"That's a relief; I haven't seen you eat anything much at all today. How often do you eat, Marvin?" "I try not to eat more than twice a day Oleather."

"Really, all I saw you eat was a small sandwich in the park and a glass of orange juice from this morning."

"Yeah, that in conjunction with your good lovin'."

"Well, I think you need to eat a little more so that you can have enough energy to give to me."

"I ordered seafood, and you will be eating."

"Is that an order?"

"It sure is, Mr. Kenyatta." They both laughed. Marvin opened the door, and Oleather smiled at the chivalrous gesture. Oleather's 2003 red convertible Dodge Stealth was a pretty sight and comfortable too.

"Nice ride Oleather. I was so into you last night that I did not pay much attention to your ride."

Unusual for a guy, Oleather thought. "Thanks, Marvin, I try." She giggled. "Marvin, I am so happy to be here with you."

"So am I, Oleather, so am I."

"You know, sweetie, I am so going to miss you when you leave tomorrow."

"I'll miss your fine ass like crazy too, but let's not dwell on that; let's enjoy what we have now and build memories for those lonely nights to come." Marvin leaned over and gave Oleather a peck on the neck, and she squealed with delight. She took Marvin's hand, and they drove hand in hand to Blockbuster as Oleather pointed out landmarks and beautiful sights and historic buildings.

"Oleather, I'd like to suggest a movie, if you don't mind."

"Sure, what is it?"

"It's a movie called Kama Sutra, The art of Lovemaking. It's an Indian movie, but the cast speaks English. One of my homeboys recommended it to me. He said it had a great storyline."

"Sounds good! Should we get two movies then?"

"Sure, why not? Why don't you choose the other one."

"Okay, how about Eddie Murphy's Raw? We could get our laugh on, and then we could get our freak on."

"I'm with you on that."

Oleather was lying comfortably on Marvin's chest when the doorbell rang.

"Oh, that must be the delivery guy." Marvin opened the door and retrieved his wallet, but Oleather stopped him.

"Oh no, Mr., this is my treat. You are my guest, and I refuse to let you pay."

"I know how difficult it is to win an argument with you, but you must let me repay you for this generous hospitality."

"Oh, don't worry," Oleather said slyly, "you will." After Marvin tipped the deliveryman, Oleather prepared the Table for dinner, and they sat down to eat.

"So, Marvin, tell me, how is it being a Parole Officer?"

"Technically, I am still training. To be honest, I haven't gotten a real feel for it yet. Right now, I am sitting in with a senior officer."

"Is he or she any good? Is it an easy learning process?" Oleather was curious.

"From what I have gathered so far, Ms. Rodriquez is an excellent trainer. I have a lot of respect for the lady."

"Is she black or white?"

"She's a sharp black woman who has been a Parole Officer for the past nine years. I have to tell you, though, Oleather, I feel a lot more relaxed on this job than when I was working in Corporate America."

"What's so different?"

"Well, for starters, in Corporate America, the whites pretty much get the upper hand. You can't tell me it's not a race thing. The white people act uppity towards each other. The few black people who are there just try to fit in. The white groups prevail. I guess the best thing about Corporate America is, if you are fortunate enough to get a good-paying job, the money is almost always really good. The downside, you almost have to sell your soul to keep up with it.

I have also realized, Oleather, that the difference between black and white in Corporate America is that white folks have a buddy system in which they promote each other. Black people don't."

"That's pretty much everywhere in America."

"I know, as unfortunate as it is."

Oleather and Marvin finished dinner and decided to take a bubble bath before sinking into their rented movies. They took turns washing each other's backs. They laughed and drank their wine while listening to Anita Baker do her thing in the background. Marvin, unable to resist Oleather, got on top of her and kissed and caressed her body passionately. They got so involved that they did not realize the water was messing up the bathroom floor. They instinctively got up and dried each other off. As Oleather led Marvin to the bed, he complied without hesitation. They did not reach the bed properly when they began groping each other as if they had minutes before the world ended.

"Oh, Marvin, I am going to miss you. You are spoiling me."

"I can say the same thing, honey. You are so good to me." As they fell on the bed, Oleather grabbed Marvin's head and guided it between her thighs. She moaned with great pleasure as Marvin used his tongue to send shivers all over her body. After reaching her climax, Oleather pushed Marvin's head away and forced him to stand up while she returned the favor. Oleather pleasured Marvin's manhood to the point of no return. Marvin tried to hold back his orgasm; He wanted to keep the feeling going, but Oleather was too good. He exploded, grabbing Oleather's head in ecstasy. Marvin pushed Oleather onto the bed and turned her over. Oleather, right on cue, positioned herself in the "doggie style" position, giving Marvin what he wanted. They rocked in harmony as they simultaneously succumbed to the passion they had created.

Exhausted, they both fell asleep with Oleather's head on Marvin's chest. It seemed as though they were sleeping for no more than a couple of hours when Marvin's tongue awoke Oleather in her ears.

"Oh honey, you can't get enough of me, can you?"

"You got it." They continued where they had left off the night before. Marvin rubbed between Oleather's thighs until, once again, she was begging for him to enter her. They made love for forty minutes, and then together, they took a long hot shower.

"Marvin, I don't want you to leave."

"Don't worry; I'll be back next month."

"But next month seems so far away."

"I know, but we will be talking lots on the phone."

"Somehow, Marvin, it doesn't seem to be enough. I need your love beside me every day."

"Love, I wish I had more comforting words for you. However, all I can say is patience is a virtue. Our love will have to stand the test."

"All I am asking of you, Marvin, is to be faithful to me."

"Oleather, I promise you, I will be faithful. You are all I want. If I haven't been sure of anything in my life, I am sure of this."

"May I have your attention, please? Continental Flight 467 is now seating passengers in rows 10 through 20. Please have your boarding passes ready to show the gate attendant."

"I guess that would be me, huh?"

"I guess so," Oleather said sadly. They hugged each other, and Marvin kissed Oleather. Tears rolled down Oleather's eyes, and Marvin wiped them.

"Hey, it'll be okay. I'll call you when I get in. I love you. Be careful going home."

"I love you too, Marvin. Have a safe trip, and I'll be praying for your safe return."

"Thanks, be strong, okay?"

"Okay, bye Marvin." They hugged again, and Oleather watched as Marvin disappeared onto the plane.

Oleather was not asleep at 10:40 pm when the phone rang. "Hello, Marvin?" Oleather said without thinking.

"Hi honey, yes, it's me, and how did you know?"

"I could not stop thinking about you... about us and the great time we had."

"Well, if it's any consolation, I am looking forward to getting together with you again soon. God, I miss you so much already. I was already thinking about a date for next month because I will be there next month without a shadow of a doubt. You have a good night, and I'll talk with you tomorrow, okay honey."

"Okay, Marvin. You've made me feel a lot better. Goodnight."

Pull Me Up

Oleather had her office door closed and had just finished talking to Marvin when a knock was on her door. "Come in; it's unlocked." Theresa walked into Oleather's office.

"Have a seat, Theresa."

"Seems like you have a serious attitude with me, girlfriend. What's up? Your man did not fuck up before he went back to Houston yesterday, did he?"

"On the contrary, Marvin was the best thing that happened to me since I moved."

"So, what's the problem then?"

"Theresa, it was easy for me to temporarily put what happened on the day of my move behind me because of Marvin's visit. Now I need to address it because underneath it all, it is bothering me, Theresa. I have known you too long and loved you too much to let this hamper our relationship. I need you to answer me honestly. Theresa, why the hell did you put me in the position you did two Saturdays ago? You know, the whole Joe incident."

"Oleather, do you mind if I get a cup of coffee before we go into this?" Theresa was calm but worried.

"Fine, get your coffee, and let's finish this. I want you to know in advance, Theresa, everything I will be saying to you is out of my love for our friendship. Since Larry is out of the office today, I am in charge, and I think this is a very good time to do this."

"Go, girl"

"Theresa, just stop the bullshitting, get your shit, sit your ass down and let's talk."

"Alright, alright, shit," Theresa said before leaving to get her coffee. She could not help noticing how angry Oleather was, but she was determined to stay as calm as she could.

"Why did you give Frank's cousin the impression that I was going to fuck him, Theresa? What the hell? Coming into my house and dropping his pants. Just because the nigga's got a big dick doesn't mean shit to me. I suspect you had a lot of influence on this. I guess you thought if you and Frank disappeared to get your fuck on, that would be a hint for me and Frank's so-called cousin?"

"Oleather, that had nothing to do with it. Oleather, you know how I am; I don't hold back shit. I was feeling horny, and I did what only I would do under the circumstance."

"Okay, I am not talking about that; my problem is you giving people the impression that I am a fucking clothespin; squeeze my head, and my legs will open."

"Listen to me, Oleather Rae, you have to believe me; I did not tell Joe any such thing. Joe can be very ignorant at times, and the alcohol only assisted in his madness. Frank spoke with Joe, and he was very embarrassed. He said he never wanted to face you again because he felt like shit."

Had I Only Known

"Theresa, I will expect you to make better calls in the future. I don't want any stupid-ass motherfuckers around me or my house."

"I understand, Oleather, and I am sorry."

"You have to be more careful with whom you deal with. AIDS has no respect for who it inflicts its death sentence upon."

"Girl, I know I act crazy as hell, and I talk lots of shit, but when it comes to sex, I am prepared. Frank and I have been dating for a while. He's no stranger to me. We are comfortable with each other."

"That's my point, Theresa, then why the hell did you think I would fuck a stranger? I am beginning to have second thoughts about the sincerity of our friendship. I heard all you said, but I still think, if you had said things differently, Joe would not have gotten the impression he obviously did."

"Oleather, you know I love you and would not do anything intentionally to hurt you. I'm sorry for the pain I have caused you. Okay, it's true, I knew what was happening, but I thought it would make you happy. Frank's cousin came across as very nice. I have never known him to act the way he did."

"Theresa, you can be clueless sometimes. Listen, I have standards that I live up to. I do this to earn the respect I know I deserve. Yeah, I play around and shit, but as you get older, Theresa, you see things differently. I have been gone for a few years now, and now that I'm back, I'm a little different, more responsible, and focused. I wish I could rub off on you."

"Oleather, I am so very sorry. I respect who you are and what you have become. I haven't now and never will judge you. I love you, and I look up to you. Please let us start over, and if you don't mind, I would like you to 'pull me up whenever you think it's necessary. I really would appreciate the guidance."

"Look, Terri...."

"You haven't called me that in a very long time. I like it."

"...I don't want to change you; you just need to polish up a bit. I still love your crazy ass. Just make sure you always have my back because, girlfriend, I will not let anyone fuck over you if I have anything to do with it." Oleather gave Theresa a big hug, and they mutually decided to start on a new note. Theresa wiped a few tears from her eyes, and they planned on lunch.

"So, how was the weekend?" Theresa inquired at lunch with Oleather.

"Oh, Terri, it was one of the best times of my life. I am so in love with this man. We talked, made love, talked, made love, and then made love some more."

"Oleather, I am very happy for you. In addition to that, girl, I am proud of the person you are. Marvin seems to be very nice and not to mention ambitious. Girl, I think this is it for you."

"He really is Theresa."

"Okay, enough about all that. How in the hell was the sex girl?"

"It was the absolute bomb. Every time I think about him, I get warm and tingly all over."

"So, you are telling me, you guys stayed most of the time indoors and fucked like rabbits?"

"Pretty much so. Girl, he is a full package. Looks good, dresses good, ambitious with a good job, and knows how to fuck his head off and eat some pussy."

"Girl, I am so glad for you... even though the man is a thousand miles away, and you have to wait to get some once a month."

"Don't be hating, girl. It's all good. As a matter of fact, it's worth the wait."

"I admire you, Oleather; you know what you want out of life, and I wish you all the best."

"Thanks, Terri; I know you mean every word of it. I want you to know that I am behind you and will be pushing you to finish up those college courses."

"I will, Oleather, really. Look, I've got lunch, okay? It's the least I can do in repentance for my sins."

"Thanks, girl, go thy way and sin no more." They both laughed then headed back for the office.

Soaring Imagination

Marvin picked up the phone before it stopped ringing. "Hey Marvin, it's me, Oleather. How are things?"

"What's up, my love? Things are good. How about you?"

"Nothing much going on, just wanted to hear my baby's voice. I couldn't stop thinking about you so, I decided to do the next best thing compared to your company."

"That's sweet, honey, and coincidentally, you were on my mind too. Oh, by the way, I don't mind you calling me baby."

Oleather laughed at his wit, "Funny, Mr. Kenyatta, what were you doing when I called?"

"I just got through eating dinner and was reading the newspaper while the Tele watched me. How about you? Have you had dinner yet?"

"Not yet, but I felt like cooking today, so I baked some fresh rolls, and I am going to make some vegetable fried rice with sweet peas and carrots on the side."

"Sounds delicious girl, you are about to stir up the neighborhood with that down-home cooking."

"You are such a first-class flatterer, Marvin." They both laughed.

"Seriously though, Oleather, I wish I could drive on over for dinner and dessert."

"Umm-hmm, so do I."

"Oleather, I have to tell you, honey, I did have the time of my life when I spent the weekend at your house. It was so beautiful; you know what I mean? I can't remember the last time I felt so whole. So complete."

"Baby, we are in sync. I know we have confessed our love for each other before, but I know now for sure that I am 100% in love with you, Marvin Kenyatta. When you were here, I had this idea of not letting you leave Charleston; it crossed my mind several times, but I had to put my selfish inclinations on the shelf and let you go back to Houston. I took comfort in the fact that sooner or later, we will be together in the same house with no distance to rob us of our togetherness."

"You know Oleather, to be honest with you, all along, I knew that there was something there between us. I think, initially and unknowingly, I was in love with the idea of being in love with you. I was in love with the way you talked on the telephone, your laugh, and your feistiness, but now, I guess all that combined with our magical lovemaking, I, like you, am sure, without any doubt, that I am in love with you inside and out. Oleather Ellis, you complete me."

"Oh, Marvin, you have made my entire life. Have you ever been married before Marvin?" The question seemed to come out of nowhere.

"No, I have never been married, but I was engaged once."

"What happened?" Oleather inquired rather curiously.

"We weren't ready."

"You or her?"

"Us; I say us because neither of us can assume the responsibility fairly. Fortunately, though, we realized that we were not compatible enough to make the big step, and we did it before it was too late. How about you Oleather, have you ever tied the knot or jumped the broom?"

"Yes, as a matter of fact, I was in a marriage for five years."

"Were you happy, Oleather?"

"I honestly was Marvin. I was happy for the first three years, and then things started to go downhill from there. I guess it would be safe to say we grew apart and there was no pulling us together again."

"That's unfortunate."

"Well, instead of making each other's lives miserable, we decided to get a divorce. The good thing, I guess, is that no children were involved."

"Do you mind if I ask about the straw that broke the camel's back?"

"Of course not; he was caught red-handed cheating on me with my best friend."

"Oh Oleather, I am so sorry. I know that was extremely hard to deal with. With that in perspective, would you consider getting married again, or was the experience so bad you don't want to repeat?"

"On the contrary, my darling, I miss being married. I love coming home to my man. It took me over two years to adjust to being by myself. There were many nights when I cried myself to sleep. I wondered what I had done wrong, what I could have done to prevent things from spiraling downwards the way it did, etcetera."

"Many people don't quite understand how emotionally difficult it is to recuperate from a divorce. It's not only the financial strain it can put on an individual, but it's mostly the separation from someone you have loved and lived with for so long... it's just tough, and I'm sorry you had to go through that. I'll mend your heart, though. That's a promise."

"You know Marvin, there were some lessons in the situation for me; I have learned a lot about myself in the last two years. I read a lot of self-help books, and I have become a very different person. I look at things in another light. I like to have fun, but I also know how to respect other people's feelings. I have learned how to make certain sacrifices in order to make things work."

"Now that we have gone all the way, Oleather, I am in it for the long haul."

"So am I, Marvin. I have to ask you though, what is it that you like the most about me? Is it the sex?"

"Well, yeah – it's definitely the sex! Just kidding, Oleather, you are a package, and I love all of you wholly and solely. I love the sex, your body, your mind, and your beautiful face. Oh, and that smile is to kill for. I love you, girl, all of you." Oleather smiled, and they were quiet for a while.

"Marvin, I have to admit, sometimes I get a little worried. I know people will cross our paths daily, and temptation will be a part of our lives, but being so far from each other is such a trial. This will be a major test of our love and commitment. Do you think we will be able to handle it?"

"Well, speaking for myself, I know you are it for me, Oleather. There is no one else in the world for me. I feel that in my heart so, the temptation will be just what it is, temptation. I can handle it. How about you?"

"I pretty much feel the same way. I think I have found my Knight in Shining Armor. No one else compares."

"On another note, how's the job assignment coming along, Oleather?"

"I like it; I like it a lot. No one looks over my shoulder anymore. My supervisor is very cool. I don't have any complaints. You know Marvin, as much as I love my job though, I would love to take a break from Corporate America and do my own thing."

"Really? That's interesting. What have you been thinking about doing?"

"I have this thing for writing so, I was thinking about maybe becoming a publisher for children's books. I would also like to do some writing of my own. I love books."

"Then, if you are serious, I'd suggest getting started on the research. You might want to start at the library researching all you can on starting a publishing company. You might also want to see if a publisher in Charleston would allow you to interview them about their business and how they got started. Of course, you won't let them know your intentions. You may want to conveniently use the student research approach, as people are very hesitant to share the reason for their success."

"Marvin, major magazines report annually that African American businesses earn lots of money, but unfortunately, in most cases, the money does not stay in the community; it goes out as fast as it comes in."

"Yep, you are right, but you are just going to focus on your business. You can make a difference and be a positive example for the rest to follow. That will give you the edge you'll need to be successful."

"Thanks, Marvin. I love learning different things about you. You are my inspiration, and I love you."

"I love you too, Oleather. Have a good night."

One Helluva Party

Marvin had stopped at a red light when he heard a horn honking. Marvin looked over and saw Isaac waving. "What's up, Marvin?"

"Yo bro, what's up? Pullover." Marvin yelled. The light turned green, and Marvin changed lanes and followed Isaac as he pulled into a strip center. Marvin and Isaac embraced each other.

"Where have you been, man? I haven't seen you in about three months."

"Man, I've been busy as hell. I started a new job, just about three months ago, as a parole officer, and they've been keeping my ass on the run."

"Shit, I thought you had left town without letting a brother know."

"Naw man, just the job."

"I'm happy for you, man. That's all good."

"Don't know bout' all that, but it's cool. I do see some shit daily. So, what you been up to, Isaac?"

"Nothing too much. I'm fixin' to head back to my apartment. Say, what are you doing later? Want to hang out at the crib? We could chill like old times then hit the club."

"No shit, which club?"

"Sodom and Gomorrah – you know, sin city."

"Sounds like life on the edge. That club is on the north side, isn't it?"

"Sho Nuff."

"Cool, I'll meet you at the crib around nine tonight?"

"A'ight." Marvin and Isaac exchanged cell phone numbers and parted ways.

As Marvin and Isaac pulled up at the club, they noticed that the line to get in was getting longer. They paid $20.00 and entered. Once they got inside, the music was pumping. People were gyrating and having a good time to the song "Back that thing up" by Juvenile. There were naked women of all origins parading around, giving lap dances to all types of men. Marvin could not remember the last time he saw so many naked butts in one place. He was in awe. Men were touching and kissing the dancers' breasts, slapping their butts, and some were even feeling the women's crotch. They all seemed to be enjoying themselves. Marvin wondered how many of the men were married and had their wives and children at home. Bills were strategically stuck in the women's skimpy underwear while they gyrated their crotch on the horny men's legs and groins.

"Hey Isaac, what's happening?" a voice came from close to the dance floor, but Isaac could not see who it was calling out to him.

"Over here," The voice said. It was Jesse, a friend of Isaac; Jesse was a wild one. If you looked in the dictionary next to the word "wild," a picture of Jesse would stare back at you. Jesse was a lot of fun to be with.

"What's happening, Jesse?" Isaac said as they dabbed each other.

"Pussy and ass, man." With his teeth clenched and without opening his mouth, Jesse cocked his head to the side, knitted his brow, and said, "Do you see all these pussies and asses up in here? Damn. Make a nigga' want to get buck wild. You know what I mean, guys, get his fuck on." They all laughed, and Marvin was in the middle of deciding Jesse's demeanor when Jesse interrupted,

"You gonna introduce me to your friend, man?"

"Aw shit, sorry man, where are my manners. Jesse, this is Marvin. Marvin, Jesse."

"Nice to meet you, man." They both said in unison.

"Marvin," Isaac said, "Jesse is the co-owner of this club." They shook hands.

"Listen, Marvin, if you need to get your fuck on, or even a blow job, let me know. I'll hook you up. We have rooms in the back that are private for your pleasure. Isaac knows the deal. Women suck dicks like crazy back there. We got this one white chick that just started working a few nights ago. The men call her "deep throat" The woman can work it. So, while you think about that, how about a couple of drinks?" "I'll take a glass of Hennessy on the rocks," Isaac said.

"And I'll have a Heineken." Jesse stopped a black waitress and told her to bring them the drinks.

This shit is Sodom and Gomorrah; I better hurry and get my ass up and outta' here. Marvin thought. At that time, the waitress came by and handed Marvin and Isaac their drinks. Isaac attempted to pay her, but she stopped him with a hand in the air, saying Jesse had already taken care of it.

"Thanks!"

Marvin and Isaac walked towards the backroom to get a whiff of what was going on. There were women on their knees with towels around their necks, giving men blow jobs. Jesse was also in there. A young Hispanic female was working on him. Upon seeing Marvin and Isaac, he yelled.

"Hey Isaac, that's 'Deep Throat' over there; it's the short white bitch with the big boobs." At this point, Marvin was feeling out of place. They looked across the room and saw the woman on her knees giving a Chinese man a blow job.

The Chinese man looked up at them and said with an accent, "She is good, man, really gooooood." The woman opened her eyes and looked toward where Marvin and Isaac were standing. Upon seeing Marvin, she gagged and choked as she recognized him as her parole officer. Marvin recognized Debra Brown instantly, and although the makeup somewhat disguised her, she was easily recognized.

"Ms. Brown, nice to see you," Marvin said sarcastically. "I will see you at 8:30 a.m. sharp on Monday morning." Then he turned and walked out the door. This was an excellent excuse to leave this hellhole.

"Hey you, don't stop sucking, fuck that neega, and keep sucking. I'm about to cum.... hey...." Isaac followed Marvin out the door.

"What's up, man?"

"Aw man, 'Deep Throat' as she is being called is one of my clients. She just got out of prison."

"Yeah, Marvin, but the bitch has a job now, man."

"Isaac, you know damn well that selling ass is not a job." "The lady has to make a living, doesn't she?"

"Obviously, we have different opinions on what constitutes employment. See, for me, selling your body is prostitution, and that's against the law."

"Hey man, chill out."

"That's a good idea. I have had enough of this Sodom and Gomorrah scene for one night. I'm sorry if I disappointed you, man; I can't stomach any more of what's going on in that club. You be careful, alright?"

"Later, my brother," Isaac said, "be careful." They embraced each other, and Isaac went back into the club.

"Marvin Kenyatta," Marvin answered the phone in his office.

"Good morning, Marvin," came the voice of the receptionist on the other end. "Your client, Debra Brown, is in the lobby to see you."

"Thanks, Ms. Jones; I'll be right out." Marvin walked to the waiting area, wondering what the expression on Ms. Brown's face would be.

"Good morning Ms. Brown," Marvin said as he signed her in on the log.

"I'll follow you to my office. You know where it is." They walked in complete silence except for the flip-flopping of Ms. Brown's slippers.

"Have a seat Ms. Brown," Marvin said as they entered the office. "How are you doing today?"

"I'm fine, thank you." Debra Brown was looking at the floor as she spoke. "Mr. Kenyatta, I am very embarrassed about...."

"Listen, we will talk about this but not right now. I'd like to ask you a few questions and get you to give a urine sample for analysis."

"Yes, sir." When Debra returned from the lab, Marvin told her to have a seat, and he closed his door to the point where there was just a crack visible.

"I am very disappointed in what I saw at that club on Friday night. You are aware that you are not to be associating with people whose character could be construed as harmful or in any disreputable environment. Are you an employee of that club?"

"Yes, sir."

"Are you licensed to dance?"

"No, sir."

"Would you like to go back to prison?" At this point, Debra was crying. Marvin could not figure out if she was crying remorsefully or just embarrassed or pissed that she was caught red-handed.

"Please, Mr. Kenyatta, please do not send me back to prison. I don't think I can ever handle going back to prison."

"You could have fooled me when I saw you Friday night. I was disgusted."

"But Mr. Kenyatta, you were there too."

"Yes, I was, and not that I need to explain myself to you, but a friend of mine took me there without me knowing what I was in for.

Seeing you was the last straw." Marvin had no intention of writing Debra up or even trying to send her back to jail. He wanted her to see how easy it was to go back to prison. Marvin remembered his initial motive when he started working for the state. He wanted to help people.

"Ms. Brown, you are young and have lots going for you. You are capable of doing many other things, based on your file, why don't you? Change is available to you. I am available to you. I can help you, but you have to want to help yourself."

"Sometimes, I just get so flustered. I am so tired of being turned down or not called back when I apply for a job."

"It's called patience and determination. I am giving you an assignment Ms. Brown; I'd like you to go to Temporary agencies, attend any job fair that comes up and apply for positions. When I see you next month, I am expecting positive results from your search, okay, Ms. Brown?"

"Yes, sir, I understand what you are saying, and I know I need to try. Thanks for being available, and thanks for caring." Marvin walked Ms. Brown to the lobby, and she smiled as she left. Marvin felt as though he was on his way to accomplishing what he initially set out to accomplish.

Searching for Answers

"Good morning, everyone!" Greeted the tall, bald white man. "Most of you know who I am, but for those of you whom I haven't met, I'm Thomas Keeper, President of the People's Accounting Firm. I am here to inform you that our company has merged with Financial Matters and we will be downsizing starting next month. I am very sorry that I have to come to you with this sad news."

There was a very brief moment of silence in the conference room where the meeting was being held, then came the chatter. Mr. Keeper continued, "I would love to keep all of you with the company, but the merge would not allow for all employees from both companies to stay. Those employees who have been with PAF for over ten years will get the opportunity to keep their jobs. For those of you who do not qualify, it is with deep regret that you will receive written notification and a compensation check. I would like you all to know that if it weren't for your hard work, this company would not be where it is today. Today, I would like to thank you all for your invaluable services. May your future be bright and rewarding. Thank you."

"I know this shit was going to happen sooner or later," Theresa told Oleather.

"Look, T, I feel bad for the others, but we are fortunate; we have given this company over fifteen years of our life and experience; we're in."

"I know, Oleather, but look at how many people will lose their jobs."

"I know, but you really should not worry about it too much. As unfortunate as it is, you still have yours."

"I know Oleather. It's just sad."

"Hey, listen, I have been thinking about starting up my own business. Maybe you can help me to get started. I'll hire you."

"Doing what?"

"Well, I have been thinking about starting my own publishing company."

"What will you be publishing?"

"Children's books." "When did you come up with this publishing idea?" Theresa asked. "I have been thinking about this for quite a while now, but last night while talking to Marvin, I think this is my calling."

"Will he come up with some of the money to get it started?"

"Girlfriend, this is my goal, my dream. I don't need to ask Marvin to help me. I have the finances to do it myself."

"I admire that about you, Oleather. When I grow up, I want to be just like you." Oleather rolled her eyes at Theresa.

"I will need you to start doing some research at the library for me, Terri. Just get information on starting the business."

"I sure will. You are very serious about this, aren't you?"

"You see what just happened in the office? Our jobs are never guaranteed so, are you down with me?"

"I'm down, Oleather. Let me know what you need me to do, and I'll do it."

"Great, thanks, Theresa."

"I'll go to the library this weekend and give you my findings over lunch on Monday. How's that?"

"Perfect, thanks, girl, we'll be alright."

"What are you going to be doing in the meantime, Oleather?"

"Well, I am going to call around to some publishing companies and try to get in on an interview with the president of the company."

"You go, girl." Theresa and Oleather embraced each other and vowed to "make this thing" happen.

Oleather was hell-bent on getting her project up and running as soon as possible. When the receptionist answered the phone, "Jack's Publishing Company." Oleather replied, "Hello, my name is Oleather Ellis, and I am a student at the University of South Carolina. I am writing a paper on how to start a publishing company, and I'd like to know if anyone there will be able to assist me with my project."

"Ms. Ellis, can you hold, please?"

"Yes, thank you." Oleather held the phone and felt a tinge of nervousness.

"This is Mr. Smith," came the voice on the other line "how may I assist you?"

"Yes, sir, my name is Oleather Ellis, and I am an English major at the University of South Carolina. I am writing a paper for my English Composition class on how to establish a publishing company. I hear that your company is a very respectable publishing company and it came very highly recommended. Since my grades are a number one priority, I wanted to get my information from the best."

"Well, I am very impressed. I will be delighted to speak to you. I am the President of this publishing house. Would you like to stop by my office next Monday morning around 10:00 a.m.?"

"If your schedule permits, I would like to treat you to lunch. Are you a seafood lover?"

"I love seafood."

"Great, I'll meet you at your office at 11:30 a.m."

"Thank you, sir, for your time, and I'll see you next Monday. Oh, Mr. Smith?"

"Yes" "would it be okay for me to bring my tape recorder as it will be easier than taking notes?"

"Absolutely. Not a problem at all."

"Thank you, sir. Goodbye." Just as Oleather hung up the phone, it started to ring. "Oleather Ellis."

"Hi Oleather, it's Theresa. Are you going out for lunch today?"

"Girl, I am going to have to pass on lunch today. I just got off the phone with the president of Jack's Publishing Company. I am so excited, Terri; I could cry. I have a lunch meeting with him next Monday to interview him about starting a publishing company. I know this is not going to be a mistake. I feel it in my bones."

"Jack's Publishing Company. Isn't that the black-owned publishing company downtown?"

"You got it, girl."

"I am so damn proud of you, girl; you sure don't waste no time."

"Are you working tomorrow?"

"I don't think so. Tomorrow being Friday, I think I'll get a head start on some research of my own and start jotting down some questions for Mr. Smith. I told him I was a student about to write an English paper."

"Why'd you lie to him, Oleather?"

"Well, I did not want to tell him that I was starting up my own publishing company, and I was stealing some of his ideas."

"Oh, girl, you are too slick. That makes sense. Okay, well, let me know how your research is going, and I'll do the same."

"Sounds good. I am still going to try to meet with some other publishing companies so, and I have lots to do."

"Okay, girl, I'm going to grab a bite. Catch up with you later."

Monday morning seemed to come around pretty fast. It was 11:20 a.m. Oleather pulled up in front of Jack's Publishing Company and parked. She walked through the revolving glass door and to the receptionist's desk.

"Hello, may I help you?" The beautiful young lady behind the desk said.

"Yes, ma'am, I'm here to see Mr. Smith."

"Yes, ma'am, he's expecting you. His office is the second brown door to your right. Please go on in." Oleather walked over to the office and knocked on the door.

"Please come in."

"Mr. Smith?"

"Yes, you must be the student."

"Yes, sir, I am Oleather Ellis."

"Very nice to meet you, Ms. Ellis." Mr. Smith stood up and extended his hand to Oleather. "Please have a seat." Mr. Smith was a distinguished-looking black man with salt and pepper hair and dark glasses. He somehow reminded Oleather of a principal. He was neatly dressed and, not forgetting, totally coordinated. Oleather was unaware that Mr. Smith was blind.

"You know Ms. Ellis; I feel the need to eat before I start all this here talking."

"Sure, Mr. Smith. I'm a tad bit hungry myself."

"Great then, I'll have one of my drivers take us over to the restaurant." The driver parked the car in front of the office, and a young black man came to Mr. Smith's office to escort him to his car. That was when Oleather realized Mr. Smith was blind. Mr. Smith was a very humorous man, and Oleather felt as though she had known him for ages.

They arrived at the restaurant, and Mr. Smith insisted the driver-assisted Oleather out of the vehicle first before he attended to him. The young driver escorted Mr. Smith and Oleather into the restaurant and left. He knew the routine. Mr. Smith would call him when he was ready to be picked up. Oleather ordered for herself and Mr. Smith. He was particular with what he wanted to order.

They talked and laughed as though they had known each other for a while. It was apparent Oleather was comfortable. She felt that Mr. Smith was going to be good company.

"Can we start our interview now, Mr. Smith?"

"Of course, shoot." Oleather dove into the questions she had prepared, and Mr. Smith answered with obvious experience and intelligence. Mr. Smith talked into Oleather's recorder, and Oleather was elated with the information she received.

"Fifty years ago, after I had just graduated from Tuskegee Institute in Alabama, my main goal in life was to become a master printer; that's what I went to school for. My father sold half of his land to buy me a building and a printing machine to start my company. My father was very supportive of my ambition. You see, Ms. Ellis, my father, and Mr. Brook T. Washington went to high school together. They did not believe in working like slaves for no white folks. I moved to Charleston to be near my oldest brother Wommie and his wife Betty until I got on my feet. Once my father finalized his sale and got the funds from the bank, he came here and bought me the building where I am today. My father had great faith in my talent as a printer, and he pushed me to build my dream."

"Was it difficult to get started? And do you still have some of your first work?

"Actually, I do. You are welcome to take a look when we get back."

"Thank you."

At that time, the waitress came by and placed their drinks on the table. Mr. Smith grabbed his glass and took a long drink. "Just what the doctor ordered." He said, smiling. His strawberry margarita was made precisely to his liking.

"Are you sure?" Oleather mused. After a brief pause, Mr. Smith continued, "Once my business began to grow, I then started publishing books by black authors."

"Why only black authors?" Oleather asked seriously.

"You see, Ms. Ellis, blacks were the only ones supporting my business. They gave me the work, and I printed it for them. They helped me establish my business, and I helped them to become published authors in return. Back then, in the early 1900s, not too many white publishing houses printed work done by black writers here in Charleston. I published a poetry book titled "Alone I Stand" by a young black and ambitious man. The people loved that book, and I started receiving manuscripts from all over. I had no idea we had so many talented black writers in our community."

"Do you still limit your publishing to black authors?"

"No, my dear, the time has changed, and you have to change with the time to stay in the running." He laughed and continued, "I publish any and everybody's work that is brought to my business." Just then, the waitress came by with Mr. Smith and Oleather's order. It looked appetizing. Oleather had ordered blackened Opelousas with a side of fried shrimp, and Mr. Smith's order consisted of grilled shrimp, grilled salmon, and oysters in a fondue sauce.

"Hmmm," Mr. Smith said, "this smells wonderful." Oleather started to move the food-filled plates around for Mr. Smith when he told her not to worry.

"I can handle this, it's one of my favorite times of the day, so I've got this down packed." They laughed, and Oleather continued with her questioning as they ate.

"What would you say the key to your success is Mr. Smith?"

"Honestly, I would have to say doing the best job for someone. You have to put one hundred and ten percent of your heart and time into your endeavors. Haphazardly doing a job will only bring you down. People talk, and once the word gets out, good or bad, that will determine the length of your existence in any business." After some more discussion, Oleather felt very assured and even more determined to continue what she had started. After they ate, Mr. Smith called the driver, and they went back to the print shop. Then Oleather departed. She planned on calling Theresa and giving her an earful of what had just transpired. Oleather was elated and motivated beyond words.

"Theresa, hey, it's Oleather. Boy, do I have a lot to tell you? I had the most wonderful day...."

Things Begin to Happen

"Hi, sweetheart," Marvin said, trying to fold his laundry and talk at the same time.

"Marvin, I am so happy you are home. I have so much to tell you."

"Girl, you sound excited as hell. Did you win the lotto?"

"No, but that'll be cool. First things first, how are you?"

"I'm fine, honey; what up?"

"Now, where should I begin? First off, the People's Accounting Firm is merging with Financial Matters company, and of course, they are downsizing. Exactly 8,000 employees will lose their jobs next month."

"Oh no, Oleather! I am so sorry to hear that," Marvin exclaimed, "What are you going to do?"

"Well, fortunately, it does not affect me. You see, if you have been with the company for ten years, you're safe. I do feel bad for the others, especially the ones that were close to their tenth anniversary."

"That's awful."

"Anyway, I know I have been with the company for 15 years, but the entire situation was an eye-opener for me. Remember what we were talking about the other night?"

"Hmm, we talked about a lot of things. We talked about me rubbing my hard...."

"Marvin, cut it out; I'm serious. We also talked about me starting my own publishing company."

"Yes, honey, what's going on?"

"Well, like I was saying, I have decided not to put all my faith in this company anymore."

"That's my sweetie; create your destiny."

"Marvin, my first grand step towards creating my destiny was to meet with the President of Jack's Publishing House here in Charleston. He was a very helpful and sincere older gentleman with a lot of passion for his publishing company."

"Did you tell him you were on your way to becoming a publisher?"

"Of course not; I told him that I am a student and that I was writing a paper for my English composition class. But I have to admit; I wished I had told him the truth. I truly believe he would have respected me for what I was trying to achieve. He told me how he got started. How his father had faith in him and how he funded the building and equipment for him."

"Oleather, I can't tell you how proud I am of you. You are a very determined individual, and it's excellent quality, a quality I admire the most about you. Keep up the good work and stay at a workable pace. You want to do it right. Of course, you'll have stumbling blocks in your path, but you'll overcome those once you stay focused."

"Thanks, Marvin. Your support means the world to me."

"You are welcomed, and I'll always be by your side."

"So, Mr. Kenyatta, what's been going on in your neck of the woods?"

"Work's great! I have been thinking about joining the YMCA to get back in shape."

"Marvin, my temperature is rising... keep talking like that boy, and you'll be sorry."

"Girl, you crazy as hell." They both laughed.

"Marvin, I don't know if I have told you this before, but I am very proud of you too."

"Thanks, honey. If you need assistance with anything at all; research, finance, whatever, would you promise to let me know?"

"I promise. Love you."

"Love you too. Bye, Oleather."

The Art of Survival

Getting paid once a month was giving Marvin the blues. Marvin felt as though as soon as he got paid, it was gone. Marvin was online looking at his checking account and thinking about how broke he was. That was the only downfall about his job, though; he loved that the benefits with the State were a lot better than his previous job. He had 14 paid holidays a year, fewer deductions from his paycheck for health insurance, and good pension benefits. "Damn, I feel like I'm on welfare and shit after I get paid once each month," Marvin said out loud. Marvin's mind shifted to one of his first conversations with Ms. Lee when he started working for the state. *Boy, was she right,* Marvin thought. "I need to look for a part-time job, and today is the best day to do it since it's a state holiday. I'm getting my ass up and out of here." With that, Marvin got out of bed and started making preparations for his next move. Marvin was very good with computers; he was a computer analyst at his previous job, and he decided to try his hand at it again on a part-time basis.

Marvin filled out several applications and was surprised when he got an immediate interview at Southwestern Bell for an Information Technician. They were hiring a few Techs for their Internet Help Desk. Marvin was prepared. He was well dressed in job-hunting attire and had his current resume with him. The interview went well, and Marvin left feeling confident. They needed techs to work on weekends, and since their techs were there 24 hours a day, Marvin could choose his hours. This was right up Marvin's alley.

It was a hot Tuesday midday, 95 degrees and getting hotter, it seemed. Marvin had just gotten through with lunch when his cell phone rang. "Mr. Kenyatta?"

"Yes, this is Marvin Kenyatta. Can I help you?"

"Mr. Kenyatta, this is Mr. Khan with Southwestern Bell Telephone Company. You interviewed for a position in our Tech department. I was wondering if you are still interested in the position?"

Marvin could not believe his ears. "Yes, sir, I am still interested in the position."

Great! We were very impressed with your background, and the interview went exceptionally well. We do not doubt that you will be an asset to our company. Can you stop by our offices on Thursday for a physical? We have a clinic on site."

"Yes, sir, I can be there during my lunch hour."

"Great, I'll see you at 11:30 a.m. on Thursday." Marvin was so excited. The job paid $23.00 an hour, and he would be averaging 16 to 24 hours per week with every other weekend off if he chooses.

It was 11:15 a.m. when Marvin arrived at the SWBT offices. He looked around at the familiar surroundings and felt a tinge of nervousness. Marvin was never too keen on Doctors' offices, even if it was not in the hospital.

"May I help you, sir? You look a bit lost." Marvin turned around and came face to face with a middle-aged black woman. She was professionally dressed, and her makeup was no less than perfect.

"Umm, yes, please, ma'am. I am trying to find my way to the clinic; I have an 11:30 appointment for a physical."

"I can help you." Marvin got directions from the lady then left. He walked into the clinic and signed the log sheet positioned on the window's sill in front of a nurse assistant.

"Mr. Kenyatta, please have a seat, fill out this form, return it to me, and we'll call you in a moment."

"Thank you." Marvin picked up a Sports Illustrated magazine on the table next to where he sat and started thumbing through the pages. It was not ten minutes later when a short white nurse came through the door looking over her glasses, "Mr. Ken-yatta?"

She had difficulty pronouncing his name, "Yes, ma'am."

"Please follow me." Marvin followed Ms. Grossman into a small room. She took his blood pressure and asked him a few questions. Marvin was beginning to feel comfortable. After writing a few notes on the form she had prepared, she told Marvin to wait, and the doctor would be in shortly. Kenny Rogers and Dolly Parton's "Island in the stream" softly came through the overhead speakers. Marvin's thoughts went to the times he would go fishing with his grandfather. He smiled to himself and decided to call Oleather. As he was reaching for his cell phone, there was a knock on the door.

"Come in," Marvin said.

"Mr. Kenyatta, I am Doctor McClendon. How are you today?"

"Just fine, thank you!" Marvin replied.

"Great! This is not going to take very long. I'll probe you in a few places, then I'll send you for a urine sample, and that's it." Marvin was given a little plastic cup for his urine. He submitted the sample to the lab technician and left.

"Hey Oleather, honey, sweetheart, how are you?"

"Boy, oh boy, you are in a good mood. My turn to ask if you won the lotto."

"Oh Oleather, there's only one of you. Guess what?" before she could answer, Marvin continued, "You know last Friday was a state holiday here in Houston, right?"

"Yes, you were off."

"Yep, and I decided to go out and look for a part-time job."

"You did? How come you didn't mention it to me before now."

"Well, I wanted to find a job before telling you. And I got called for a position with SWBT. I'll be working as many hours as I want on weekends, and they are paying me $23.00 an hour. What do you think?"

"That's great, Marvin, but you are going to work yourself sick."

"Not really; I'll be a helpdesk technician, so it's not too much running around. Actually, it's pretty much what I was doing at PAF."

"How about our weekends together?" Oleather had genuine concern in her voice.

"Not a problem honey, I get every other weekend off if I choose to. Also, I'll have the option of switching with one of my colleagues if need be."

"Sounds like it all fell together in a positive way for you."

"Sho did."

"Well, I am happy for you. I know you have been complaining about being paid once a month. That's a hard thing to do, so I am very excited for you."

"Thank you, sweetie pie."

"Listen, I'm pulling up to the office, so I'll call you later, okay, love?"

"Okay, Marvin. I love you. I can't wait for my trip to Houston to visit you."

"That's right; you'll be here soon. Uh oh, I'd better hide the G-strings and the fishnets…. just pulling your legs. You know you're the only one for me."

"I know, and I'll have to spank you when I get there."

"Spank away, baby. I love it."

Let's Keep in Touch

Marvin was on his way to Houston's Intercontinental Airport to pick up Oleather. This was the weekend Oleather was visiting, and it was also Marvin's weekend off. The night was cool, and Marvin opened the doors and the sunroof to his Limited Ford Expedition. He was jamming to R. Kelly's "Love Slide." Marvin longed for this night and was counting the days for two weeks now. He looked especially handsome. He was wearing a tight black top that showed off his beautiful chest and arms and a pair of Phat Farm blue jeans. Marvin sang along to R. Kelly, enjoying the fact that there was no traffic on the freeway. It seemed as though every time he entered the freeway, there was back-to-back traffic.

"Ladies and Gentlemen, thank you for flying American Airlines. We will be descending in five minutes...." Oleather's eyes brightened with excitement. She was very excited about seeing Marvin again. Oleather was wearing a tight pair of Guess jeans with a pink knitted halter top. She was gorgeous. She wondered if Marvin was already at the airport waiting for her or if he was late? "Nah, I know he's there." She thought and smiled devilishly at the secret plans she had for them both.

Marvin was waiting at the gate when Oleather got off the plane. Oleather could not reach Marvin fast enough. They kissed in front of everyone in the waiting area and did not give a damn.

"It is so good to see you, Marvin."

"It's good to see you too. You look great!"

"Yeah? You don't look so bad yourself, handsome." Oleather said, giggling.

"Are you hungry?" Marvin said.

"Yeah, I am starving for your loving." Marvin laughed and knew that secretly he felt the same way Oleather did.

"Do you have any baggage's to be claimed?"

"I have all that I traveled with right here with me, honey." Marvin took Oleather's handbag, and they walked hand in hand to the airport exit door. As they drove down Highway 59, Oleather could not take her hands off Marvin. Marvin reached in his back seat and retrieved a bottle of White Zinfandel wine. He already had the two glasses in the cupholder.

"Oh, so that's what those were for," Oleather purred.

"Normally, this isn't something I would ask of you but would you do the honors of opening and pouring this?"

"Actually, I don't mind at all," Oleather said as she turned up the volume on the radio. "Distant Lover" by Marvin Gaye was blaring over the radio station.

"Oh, I do love this song. It does things to me, Marvin."

"Hold that thought, sweetie." They laughed as Marvin sang along.

"Oleather, I am taking you out to dinner before we go to the apartment. What is it that your tummy desires, my dear?"

"How about some good ole' seafood? As you know, that's my favorite cuisine."

"Sounds great. We'll pull into Pappadeaux's off highway 59."

"On second thought," Oleather said, "Let's get it to go. We can eat at your apartment and not be held responsible for what happens after that."

"Sounds good; we'll do that." They got their dinner and headed for the apartment. While Marvin was preparing the table for dinner, Oleather decided to take a shower.

Phyllis Hyman's CD played when Oleather walked out of the bedroom in a pink and white nightgown. She was stunning. She was wearing a pink 3-½ inch stiletto with glass heels, and her hair was now taken out of the bun and was cascading over her shoulders. Oleather smiled mischievously at Marvin. Marvin's mouth dropped, and he looked like he had just seen an angel.

"Wow, Oleather, you look breathtaking." Oleather did look like a doll.

"Well, thanks, honey. All for you, of course, and what you see is what you get." Marvin pulled out a chair at the table for Oleather to sit, and he filled her glass with wine. They ate, talked, and laughed over dinner. After dinner, both Oleather and Marvin had one too many glasses of wine, and one thing led to the other.

"I have waited for this for a long, long, long time," Marvin said as he pulled Oleather into his arms. They were sitting on Marvin's leather couch, and Phyllis Hyman was still crooning. The atmosphere was conducive to Oleather and Marvin's environment. Oleather slowly kissed Marvin on his eyes, nose, lips, ears, and chest.

Marvin was having a difficult time concealing what he was feeling. They kissed each other passionately and eventually ended up on the carpet. Marvin's erection was so visible that Oleather was drowning in desire and anticipation. She unzipped Marvin's pants and rubbed his erection until he was begging for her this time. Marvin took off Oleather's negligee, leaving her wearing only her high heels. This time, Oleather did not ask Marvin to do what he was about to do. It was a spontaneous move when Marvin spread Oleather's legs apart. Before he could satisfy his desires, Oleather decided the time was not right by gently pushing his head away. She was in the mood to tease. Oleather cunningly got up and started dancing for Marvin. Whenever he tried to touch her, she moved away, licking her lips and gyrating her naked hips to the sounds on the stereo. As the music continued to play, she played with her breasts, lightly tugging at her nipples and touching herself ever so seductively. Marvin's eyes were wild with passion.

"Please, Oleather, let me have you now, please."

"Not yet, sweetheart, patience." she crooned. Marvin was on his knees with his hands on his erected manhood, moving it up and down. It seemed as though he was moving with the same rhythm as Oleather. Oleather then moved slowly to where Marvin was kneeling. She positioned herself where her center was over Marvin's face.

"Yes," Marvin said, "Yes, come here you." Marvin stuck out his tongue and welcomed Oleather's wetness. Marvin licked and sucked until Oleather fell onto the couch with a massive orgasm. After a few seconds, Oleather grabbed Marvin's ass, "my turn," she said as she engulfed Marvin's long thickness into the walls of her mouth. Marvin felt as though a vacuum was sucking him in, and there was nothing he could do about it. It was the best feeling, he thought.

"Don't stop." Marvin moaned, "Pleeeeeze, don't sta... sta... sta... stop." Marvin was gasping. It was not long after that Marvin exploded uncontrollably. They collapsed on each other. It was not very long after, Marvin was behind Oleather, humping her like a dog in heat. Now it was Oleather's turn to gasp. Oleather yelled Marvin's name as she reached her climax. Marvin pulled out as he moaned and released his juice on Oleather's back. They lay in each other's arms for a few minutes without saying anything.

Then Marvin said, "Oleather, honey, I think we should be protecting ourselves. I was thinking; I should wear a condom when we have sex."

"Why Marvin, why now? When you were at my place, you didn't wear one."

"Guilty as charged. I wasn't thinking, honey."

"So, what's the deal now? Do you think I'm fucking someone else? Is that it?" Oleather got defensive.

"No, Oleather, of course not! We love each other, and for both of our sakes, I think we should both get a check-up and produce negative papers. Let's start on the right track Oleather."

"You are right, Marvin. I am sorry for behaving like this. It makes sense. We'll use a condom the next time."

Oleather and Marvin got up and took a shower together. Marvin had planned on taking Oleather to the casino in Louisiana. He wanted to take her to the Grand Coushatta. It was about a four-hour drive, so they stopped at a local IHOP for breakfast. They looked so happy together, chatting and giggling, kissing and touching each other. The drive was a long and beautiful one. Oleather and Marvin got even more acquainted with each other's lives and family. Once they arrived at the Coushatta, they did not know where to begin. It was 5:20 pm when they got there. Neon-colored lights were flashing different designs throughout the large casino halls.

"Let's have a drink before we get to gambling," Marvin said. Once in there, one could not tell if it was night or day.

"I've never gambled before," Oleather said, sounding a little concerned.

"Don't you worry your pretty little head, my darling; it'll come to you like breathing."

"Sure, it will," Oleather said sarcastically, "then again, you're the pro."

"Just follow my lead, little one." Oleather pinched Marvin's behind playfully.

"Let's look at that little ole' lady over there," Marvin said. They walked over to the slot machine and stood behind the old woman as she inserted her quarter into the machine and pulled the handle at the side of the machine. "The object of the game is to get three of a kind to win. If you do what the lady just did, the machine will do the rest."

"Looks easy enough." A waitress came by in a very short skirt and offered two glasses of lemon jello schnapps. They played, and they drank, then they drank some more. Marvin insisted that Oleather did most of the playing.

"I'll get the change, and you'll play," Marvin said. Oleather was getting discouraged. She was playing and not winning until finally, as if the machine was in sync with Oleather's thoughts, it started making loud, consistent ringing sounds. "You hit it, baby, you won! You won!" People began gathering around the machine to see how much Oleather had won.

"$3,000.00 Oleather, damn girl, you did it! You really did it!" Oleather was speechless.

"I did? I did, wow hell yeah, I did it." A young black woman came over to the machine and congratulated Oleather. The machine only had $1,000 in quarters, so she handed Oleather a slip for $2,000.00 to be cashed at the front desk. Oleather could not stop kissing Marvin and thanking him for having faith in her. Oleather cashed her receipt and collected her cash in $100 bills. Without Marvin asking, Oleather split the money in half so that they could enjoy the rest of the night. Marvin knew at that moment that Oleather was his for life. They decided not to play anymore. It was 11:46 p.m., and Marvin opted to go to their reserved room.

"For $125 per night, this is not bad at all," Oleather mentioned. Their room was a suite. The suite included a kitchen and a sauna. Oleather's mind was going at rapid speed. She envisioned all the wonderful things that could be accomplished in the room before they headed back to Houston.

"Uh oh," Oleather exclaimed, "What's the matter, honey?"

"I don't have a change of panties."

"Easily fixed. We could go shopping."

"Nah, I think I'll travel back without any panties." She winked at Marvin, who seemed to be blushing.

"Marvin, winning such a big win makes me feel so great. I feel powerful... like I can conquer the world."

Marvin laughed, "I can imagine. You know, I had a feeling that you would win big tonight. Call it ESP, but I just knew it, and Bam, you did. Girl, you are some package... my package. I sure do know a winner when I see one." Oleather got closer to Marvin and hugged and kissed him.

Had I Only Known

"Let's go shopping in the morning," Marvin said.

"Sure, sounds like fun." They were so tired; they fell on the bed and were fast asleep. A knock on the door awakened Marvin.

"Room service" came the voice of a man.

"One moment," Marvin said. It was a complimentary continental breakfast the hotel served its guests at 8:00 a.m.

Oleather rubbed her eyes and sat up, "What was that?" she asked.

"Room service, honey. Hungry?"

"Sure." They had breakfast followed by an early morning Jacuzzi sex session. Oleather and Marvin got dressed and left for the mall. They decided to go swimming, so they both needed bathing suits.

Oleather was excited to see a Macy's department store. Marvin followed Oleather around as she shopped.

"I thought you only needed a bathing suit?"

"Well, now that I am here, I could pick up a few more needed items."

"Sure, honey." Oleather picked up two sundresses, a beautiful bathing suit, and Marvin got some swimming trunks. They headed back to the hotel and decided to go for a swim.

"Did you know that I was a lifeguard?" Marvin asked Oleather.

"Really, pretty impressive big daddy," she played. Marvin dove into the water and swooped Oleather up. She screamed and begged him not to throw her. Too late, Marvin picked Oleather up and threw her into the water. She splashed and got her balance in enough time to push Marvin underwater. They were having the time of their lives. Finally, all the touching and playing around got their sexual appetites going. They decided to leave the pool and settle for the Jacuzzi in their room. They made fantastic love. Marvin decided to get back into Houston before it got too dark. He wanted to spend some quality time together before Oleather's departure to Charleston.

The Restless Quest for Romance

Marvin answered his telephone, hoping he would hear Oleather's sweet voice. When Marvin answered, Oleather's perky voice came on the other end, "Hi baby, I made it home safely."

"Great, I have been praying for your safe return."

"Well, honey, your prayers were answered. Marvin?"

"Yes, Oleather."

"I just wanted to let you know that I have concluded you are a good man for me. You touch my spirit and my heart. I rejoice each time I think of you. You are one of the few men who have come into my life and touched my entire being. You make me whole, Marvin, just like a woman should feel about herself and her man."

"Baby, I know you don't like me calling you 'baby,' but I think we are now way past that. You know how genuine I am and when I call you baby, I mean it. Oleather, you also bring out the best in me. I feel so together when I am with you, and when I think about you, I can't imagine things any different; I can't imagine anyone else in my life. I adore you, honey."

"Honestly, Marvin, do you think within your heart of hearts that there's a future for the two of us?"

"With all my heart, I do."

"How long are we going to be distant lovers, baby? It's becoming more and more unbearable to not be in your strong arms when I want to."

"Not long, I hope. I thought we had been traveling back and forth to see each other for almost a year now. We both know what we want; why don't you move down to Charleston? It will be very feasible since I just bought the house out here. Of course, I'm not trying to push you, and the final decision will be yours. You can manage my company, make that our company," she corrected, "I know that working together, we can build one hell of a company and enrich our lives."

"Oleather, believe it or not, I have thought about it on several occasions but did not want to scare you. I believe we can do this together."

"Oh, Marvin, we are so on the same path." Oleather was in tears of joy.

"Marvin, I am so happy I don't know what to do with myself. I wish you could kiss me right now."

"So, do I. Actually, if I had it my way, I'd do more than kiss you." They were quiet for a few seconds; both were lost in their thoughts. Marvin imagined what it would be like not to be so far away from Oleather, and Oleather was fantasizing about coming home to Marvin every day. She wanted to get back into the routine of cooking for her man and running his bathwater.

"Oleather?"

"Yes, baby."

"Remember what we talked about; me moving to Charleston and working with you? Well, I'd like you to promise me that you'll think about it tonight. I'll do the same, and we'll talk again tomorrow. I want to let you know once again; I love you the most."

"I'll think about our conversation, but I know how I feel, Marvin. I love you, and I'll talk with you tomorrow."

"Bye sweetie, I love you too."

It was almost three and a half months since Oleather had visited Marvin in Houston. She had not been feeling very well lately. Oleather had missed her period for a few months and felt ill, especially in the morning hours. It was Saturday night, and Oleather had spoken to Marvin a few hours earlier, but she decided to call him again anyway.

"Hello? Marvin, it's Oleather."

"Hi sweetheart, you don't sound so good, are you okay? It's 1:45 a.m. what are you doing up?"

"I couldn't sleep so I decided to call you. I'm sorry for calling you so late."

"No, it's really okay. Don't you know by now you are my best friend? You, my darling, can call me at any time."

"Are you up to some news?"

"Good or bad?"

"You can decide. Marvin, I think I may be...."

"Pregnant?"

"I think so."

"You mean, you are having a baby? Our baby?"

"I have not had a period in three months, and I have been feeling ill, especially in the mornings."

"Well, have you seen a doctor yet?"

"Not yet, but I do have an appointment on Tuesday at 10:00 in the morning."

"I knew it would happen sooner or later. We did not use a condom initially, and that's a chance we took."

"Are you disappointed?"

"Disappointed? Heck no. I am thrilled to be the father of your child. We did not plan it, but that's okay. Honey, please call me immediately after your doctor's appointment on Tuesday morning, okay?"

"Yes, sir. You know Marvin, I was not afraid to tell you, a little nervous maybe about the timing."

"We don't plan for a lot of things in life, sweetie, but it comes our way, and we deal with it as such. I can't believe I may be a daddy soon. Oleather, call me on Tuesday as soon as you get your results, and we'll go from there. I love you so much, honey."

"Thanks, Marvin, I'll call, and that's a promise."

Creating your own Challenge

"Hello Mr. Williams, good morning."

"Good morning to you, Mr. Kenyatta. Did you have a nice weekend?"

"I did; thank you, sir. I am on top of the world."

"Really, may I ask what's gotten you so 'on top of the world'?"

"My girlfriend just informed me that she might be pregnant. It's wonderful news."

"I am very happy for you, Marvin. Where does your girlfriend live?"

"She's in Charleston, South Carolina. We take turns visiting each other."

"I tip my hat off to you Marvin, your phone bill must be really high."

"Not really, you know there are lots of convenient long-distance phone plans in place these days. It's not that bad at all. Besides, she's worth every penny."

"Are you thinking about getting married?"

"It's a possibility."

"Well, I hope the fact that she may be pregnant is not your motive for getting married?"

"No, sir, I love the lady unconditionally."

"That's good to hear. I'm 63 years old now, but I have done my share of sleeping in nests over the years. I did it until I was sure I had found the right nesting place, which turned out to be my wife of 42 years. If you are sure that you have hopped enough, then go for it. Give that woman everything you've got."

"Mr. Williams, I know within my heart that I am ready."

"I am very happy for you, Marvin. You are a wonderful young man, and you will do great. If she is as good to you as you are to her, your marriage will be blissful."

"Thank you, sir, you are a very kind man."

"Good luck Marvin, see you later."

"Goodbye, Mr. Williams, and thanks again." Marvin could not wipe the smile off his face; he was ecstatic about the way things were going for him. Marvin walked back to his office and thought about his conversation with Oleather the night before. He thought about moving to Charleston and was very happy about the idea. The more he thought about it, the more he was convinced that it was an excellent move. The telephone rang, and the receptionist told Marvin that his client, Johnny Walker, was in the lobby. Marvin walked to the lobby and called Johnnie Walker; he followed Mr. Walker silently down the hallway. Once in the office, Marvin greeted Mr. Walker, "How are you today, Sir?" He reached into his desk drawer and retrieved a file with 'Johnny Walker' written on it.

"I'm doing okay, Mr. Kenyatta."

"Have you gotten a job yet?"

"No, sir."

"Have you been looking?"

"Ain't no jobs out there anyway; it's a waste of time even to try."

"So, Mr. Walker, it's safe to say you haven't tried."

"Look, man; it's not easy. You have it good, so you don't know what it's like on the other end of the fence, you up here in this fancy office, making good dough; you just don't know what it's like, okay?"

"Listen to me and listen to me really well, Mr. Walker, you are on parole. You have to make an effort to get a job so that you can repay the damage that landed your butt in jail in the first place."

"I did my time, sir."

"Yes, you did, but now you need to pay for the crime. Mr. Walker, you cannot beat the system. You have two options; you either get a job fast, or you will be sent back to the penitentiary, that's it. Listen, I am not trying to tug your chains, but this is the real world; the faster you accept reality, as it is, the better for you. You have been released for over three months now, and you are not making any progress. It would help if you made a positive attempt to get your life in order. If you don't, no one will do it for you. I do not have any mercy on you anymore; you will have to show me some effort."

"You know what, send me back to prison, Mr. big parole officer. I don't give a shit."

"Now, you are acting like a hopeless ass. What is it? Can't you survive without mass whipping your ass and forcing you to do his will? Is that it? Come on, man; you are twenty-seven years old with your entire life ahead of you. Do something positive. Yes, you call me 'Mr. Big parole officer'. I know you are frustrated, but I worked my butt off to get here, man. I had to make some big sacrifices to get here. Nothing in life comes easy, and when it does, you have to question it. Look, I am here to help you, but you've got to help yourself, man. Do you want to die?"

"Whatever, I don't care."

"Well, Mr. Walker, I do care if you die. As much as you don't realize it, you can turn this thing around for the better. Please, bear with me for a little while; I will be available to you when you need me. Allow me to make a difference. I'll make some calls for job placement, and we'll go from there; what do you say?"

"You are very kind, but the answer is no; I prefer to go back to jail."

"Have it your way, Mr. Walker. I tried." Marvin picked up the phone and called his supervisor, "Ms. Stewart, I'm sorry to bother you, but can you please come over to my office. I have Mr. Johnny Walker with me. Thank you."

It was not two minutes when Ms. Stewart walked into Marvin's office. "How can I help you, Marvin."

"Ms. Stewart, Mr. Walker here has decided to go back to jail as opposed to accepting my offers to help him better his life." Ms. Stewart turned around and looked at Mr. Walker with sincere concern.

"Mr. Walker, may I ask you why you have chosen jail instead of a better life?"

"I am not doing well out here; I will be better off in prison."

"That easy, huh? Have you been paying your fees?"

"No, cause I ain't got no money."

"What have you done to get money, Mr. Walker?"

"I tried, and ain't nobody wants to hire a jailbird."

"Well, I have some news for you; I am not sending you back to jail. It is not going to be that easy. You have been in jail for the last ten years, and our job is to assist you to the best of our ability in becoming a working, productive, and law-abiding citizen just like the rest of us. This is the course of action we will take; I will assign you to a six-month group home. In this home, they have various training programs that will help you ease back into society. I want you to be serious and learn all that you can. You may come out of there and make more money than I am making. Shoot, I may be coming to you for financial help because you will be the man." Mr. Walker listened intently and seemed to be absorbing all that was being dished out.

"Are you willing to try?"

"Yes, ma'am, I will."

"Great, then can I have a handshake and a smile?" Ms. Stewart smiled back and said, "That wasn't so bad, was it?"

"No ma'am, thank you and Thank you too, Mr. Kenyatta." Ms. Stewart gave Marvin the information on the program she recommended for Mr. Walker. She then winked at Mr. Walker and walked out of the office.

"Ms. Stewart sho' is convincing," said Mr. Walker, "She's a pretty good talker too."

"Mr. Walker, she wants to help you. She sees in you what I see."

"If you have a seat in the lobby, Mr. Walker, I'll call you when a representative from the group home is here to pick you up."

"Okay, Mr. Kenyatta, thank you." They shook hands, and Marvin assured Mr. Walker that he would be praying for him and that he, along with others, cared.

On My Own

It was 1:45 p.m. when Oleather walked into Dr. Bell's office; her appointment was scheduled for 2:00 p.m. "Hi, my name is Oleather Ellis, and I have an appointment with Dr. Bell at 2:00 p.m."

"Yes, Ms. Ellis, please sign the log and have a seat; we will call you in a moment...Oh, Ms. Ellis,"

"Yes, ma'am." "Has your insurance changed?"

"No, it's still the same."

"Thank you; we'll be with you momentarily." Oleather watched an infomercial on the television screen when a pudgy Hispanic nurse poked her head out the door and called her in.

"Ms. Ellis, please follow me; I'd like to get your weight and take your vital signs before Doctor Bell come in to see you.

Oleather waited in the room for what seemed like ages before Dr. Bell knocked on the door. "Come in," Oleather said.

"Well, hello, Ms. Ellis, how are we doing today?"

"Just fine, Dr. Bell. Thanks for asking."

"How are your mom and dad doing?"

"They're both fine." Dr. Bell had been Oleather's family's physician for many years and was very familiar with Oleather's history.

"Are you still residing in Houston, Heartland?"

"No, sir, I moved back to Charleston."

"I guess your parents are delighted you moved home. Do you still have your old room?"

"Actually, Dr. Bell, I bought my home a few months ago."

"Well, good for you. I saw your dad last week, and he did not mention anything about you being back home. Talked about everything else except his pretty little girl."

"Hmm, I'll have to talk with my dad." They both laughed.

"So, Oleather, what can I do for you today?" Oleather hesitated for a moment.

"I think I may be pregnant, Dr. Bell. I want to be quite sure so that I may take the necessary precautions."

"Have you missed your period?"

"Yes, it has been three months since my last one." Oleather changed into some hospital attire and laid on her back on the small bed in preparation as instructed for Dr. Bell's examination.

"Well, Oleather, it looks like you are about to bring a little one into this world. From my examination, I'd say you are just about three months pregnant. I'd like you to give a urine sample for confirmation, but I am one hundred percent sure." Oleather was speechless for a moment. Many thoughts were going through her head. She had to tell Marvin, her mom, and her dad; she was ecstatic.

"Thank you, Dr. Bell; I am so happy. I can't wait to tell Marvin it's been confirmed."

"I will give you a prescription for your prenatal vitamins, and the nurse will talk with you about your schedule to set up an appointment for next month. Remember, no alcohol, drugs, and eat healthily."

"Oh, do not worry, I will do everything in my power to ensure the well-being of this little one. Thank you, Dr. Bell."

As Oleather left Dr. Bell's office, she found it rather difficult to contain her excitement. She smiled at almost everyone who crossed her path. As Oleather drove up to her house, two cars were parked in her driveway; one belonged to Theresa and the other, which she found out later, belonged to a printer. She heard the noise in her garage and could not imagine what was going on in there. She walked around the side; the door was opened. Oleather was amazed at what she saw. She was so delighted she let out a shriek of excitement. The printer was setting up her printing and binding machinery.

"Hey girlfriend, we are about to be in business," Theresa yelled, and they hugged each other in obvious happiness. Oleather was so happy; she had gotten two sets of good news in one day.

"When did you do this, Theresa?" Oleather asked.

"When you were in Houston with Marvin. We were fortunate to get everything used but in great working condition."

"What was the total cost?"

"$32,000 for both machines. Of course, I got a professional opinion before purchasing. This gentleman is teaching me how to run it."

"Great, I'll join you guys. You are such a sneak, Theresa. You have outdone yourself by not telling me about this. I had no idea you could hold a secret like that."

"Well, actually, I was still in the negotiations process when you came back."

"Good job. Thanks!" Oleather, unable to control her emotions any longer, started crying.

"Oleather, honey, what's wrong? Aren't you happy?"

"Yes, Terri, I am overjoyed. You see, today will go down as one of the most memorable days of my life. I will never forget today. All in one day, I found out that my company is getting off the ground and that I am three months pregnant."

"Oh, Oleather, are you serious? Oh my gosh, I am going to be an aunt. Oleather, this is great; you and Marvin are so perfect together; I can't imagine something like this happening to a better person. Oh, I love you, and I am so happy for you. Okay, you know now no lifting heavy...."

"Terri?"

"Yes, Oleather."

"Relax, I think I have it under control. I know you will be there for me when my hormones start to rage out of control."

"Girl, you know I will. By the way, does Marvin know that you are pregnant?"

"I kinda' told him before I got confirmation from the doctor."

"And?" Theresa asked wide-eyed in anticipation.

"Girlfriend, he was as happy as a man just finding out he had won the lotto."

"So, what's the next move?" Theresa asked, "You know you can't do the long-distance thing for long now?"

"Yeah, we touched the topic. Marvin said he'll start working on getting his shit together in Houston; then he'll move out here with me before the baby is born."

"Just like a nigga' to make his bitch wait until he makes a decision."

"Theresa, you are lucky that I love you and have known you forever or else... besides, I am not his bitch; I'm his lady, thank you very much."

"Or else what?" Oleather hugged Theresa affectionately

"Or else... nothing. Absolutely nothing." They laughed.

"Oh, by the way, Oleather, I trust in you so much that I resigned from my current position to give you 100%."

"Oh, Theresa, you are a good friend. We may have our ups and downs, but you are truly my sister. Anyway, I'll pay you more than what you were making."

"Good. Then, I'll get comfortable and fix us some lunch." The printer guy had left a while ago, so it was pretty quiet. Theresa went into the kitchen, and Oleather stayed in the garage. She walked around rubbing her stomach and touching the machinery.

"Little one, everything will be just fine. Can you hear me? I love you, and I can't wait to see you." Oleather stayed in the garage for about ten minutes before joining Theresa in the kitchen. They talked and talked about Oleather's unborn baby and their new venture. They made plans and promises to each other.

"Oleather, thanks for everything."

"You are welcomed, crazy friend," Oleather said, nudging her best friend on the shoulder.

Mission Completed

Oleather's heart was racing with excitement as she dialed Marvin's number. "Hi, Honey," Oleather said into the receiver.

"Oh, hi baby, how are you?"

"I'm good. You sound totally out of breath. What are you up to?"

"Oh nothing, I barely heard the phone ringing, and I was in the shower, so I raced to pick it up. Is everything okay with you? Did you go see the doctor?"

"As a matter of fact, all are very well. I did go to see Dr. Bell, and he told me that I was three months pregnant."

"Oh baby, that is wonderful news. We are going to be parents. Oleather, I am so happy for us."

"I am too, baby. Guess what else?"

"I'm scared to ask; just kidding, what's that baby?"

"My publishing company is on its way. As of this morning, we are up and running."

"That's great news, honey. When did this all happen?"

"While I was having fun with you in Houston. Theresa used the money I got from the bank. Before I went to Houston, I told Theresa to look for good equipment. You know we had done some advertising before I left. Theresa took the initiative, did some consulting with some experts then bought the needed machinery. Printing started early this morning after I had left for my doctor's appointment."

"Congratulations, baby girl, I am so proud of you. God is definitely good."

"I feel truly blessed, Marvin. My dreams are coming alive. The only thing missing is you, baby."

"Ah, Oleather, on that note, I have some news myself."

"Really? What might that be?"

"Well, baby, I gave a lot of thought to what we discussed and our future, and I have decided to give my notice to the Parole office. I am quitting being with you. Oleather, will you marry me?" Oleather started to cry. To her, this was all too good to be true, but it was true.

"Yes, Marvin, yes. I will marry you. You are the man of my dreams. I will marry you."

"Great, that settles it. I'll see you soon, honey. I so love the two of you."

"Oh, Marvin, I could get used to the sound of that."

On the Move

Marvin walked into Mr. Edmon's office. The door was opened. "Good morning Mr. Kenyatta; I received your letter of resignation on Monday and wanted to let you know that I hate to lose you."

"Good morning to you, sir."

"I thought you were happy Marvin, why are you leaving?"

"Sir, I am getting married and will be a dad soon. My fiancé just bought a house and lives in Charleston, South Carolina. I will be joining her."

"Marvin, I wish you the best of luck. I am happy for you. If you ever need anything, anything at all, please do not hesitate to contact me personally. You have been one of my best employees, and I do hate to see you leave, but I understand."

"Thank you very much, sir."

"Listen, Marvin, the other Officers and I would like to take you out to dinner a couple of days before your leaving if your schedule permits."

"Absolutely, sir, I would like nothing better." Marvin walked out of Mr. Edmon's office elated. In the hallway, he stopped by Ms. Rodriquez's office. Ms. Rodriquez had been extremely welcoming to him when he started his job at the parole office. He knocked on the door and waited for a response. "Hi there, Marvin, come on in. How's your day going?"

"Hi Ms. Rodriquez, I'm doing pretty good. Actually, I am on top of the world."

"Wow, you sound like it. What's going on?"

"Well, I am getting married, about to have a baby, and, here's the down part, will be leaving the parole office to relocate to Charleston, South Carolina."

"Whoa, hold on a minute. Are you telling me that you are quitting?"

"Unfortunately, yes."

"Marvin, Marvin, I don't want you to leave. I was just beginning to like you." She laughed. "Just kidding, you are a wonderful person, and only good things will follow you. I am happy for you, Marvin. Good luck and congratulations!"

"Thank you, Ms. Rodriquez, you were my best friend here, and I will miss you. But I will stay in touch from time to time. This is not goodbye."

"I'm happy to hear that, Marvin." With that, Ms. Rodriquez hugs Marvin.

"So, I take it you are reuniting with your Charleston lover?"

"Right on the money." Marvin mused. "Ms. Rodriquez, she's the woman I am sure I want to make my wife."

"So, who proposed, you or her?"

"I did."

"Was she ready?"

"Oh yes, she was very ready."

"Did she cry?"

"She did it all." They both laughed, and Marvin noticed that Ms. Rodriquez was genuinely sorry that he was leaving. Marvin was going to miss her the most.

"Marvin, if you let me know the big day, I'll try my very best to come up to Charleston to help you celebrate."

"Would you really do that for me, Ms. Rodriquez?"

"I most definitely will."

"Ms. Rodriquez, thank you for all you have done for me. You were my inspiration."

"Well, my dear, you made it easy because you were willing and ready to learn, and I enjoyed showing you what I knew." Mr. Alston mentioned that a couple of days before leaving, he and some other officers would be taking me out. I sincerely hope that you will be a part of the group."

"I will be there. Count on it." They hugged again, and Marvin left her office feeling a little sad. He had really gotten close to Ms. Rodriquez.

Present and Future

Oleather picked up the phone and dialed Theresa's number. "Hey girlfriend, wazzup?"

"I tell you, thanks to technology, you know who's calling."

"Hush girl, you know I gots to keep up with the Joneses and big-timers like you."

"Girl, I ain't a big timer. Just trying to make a dollar out of fifteen cents. Girl, you know we will both be blinging."

"True, because as we speak, we are bling blinging our first children's book."

"Girl, there is so much excitement going on in my life right now."

"Okay, what else am I missing, girlfriend?"

"Come on over to my place, I have much to tell you, and I do need you right now."

"Say no more; I'll be there in thirty minutes."

In forty-five minutes, Oleather's doorbell was ringing. Oleather ran to the door, checked the peephole, and opened it for Theresa. "Hey, girlfriend, with your fat self."

"To hell with you bitch, I am so not fat yet. Come on in and sit your crazy ass down." They embraced and walked towards the couch.

"Oleather, it's amazing how we can talk to each other the way we do and know secretly that it's okay; can you imagine someone on the outside listening to us? They'll probably think we have lost our minds."

"You know it!"

"So, what's going on girl, you sounded like you needed another pair of ears."

"Well, I spoke with Marvin not too long ago, and guess what?"

"What girl?"

"Marvin will be here next two weekends from now. Girl, he's moving down here with me, and guess what else?"

"Are you getting married?"

"Yes, girl, Marvin asked me to marry him."

"You did say yes, didn't you?"

"I sure as hell did. Terri, I am so happy I don't know if I should laugh or cry."

"You can do both, you know; there is no law against that." Theresa was so excited about the news; she was now on her feet, acting out her excitement like a little child.

"When is the wedding. Oh my gosh! I have so much planning to do. We have so much planning to do. We have to get the invitation lists done; we have to decide on the hall, your wedding dress, we...."

"Theresa, you are making me dizzy girl, slow down."

"Sorry, Oleather, but I am so excited, I can't contain myself."

"I can't believe that Marvin is quitting his job and moving with me to assist with our company girl."

"You are one lucky lady Oleather. I know I play around a lot, but I like what I've been saying a lot; lately, I am so proud of you. I know I have told you that before, but Oleather, I am very proud to have you as a sister."

"Well, sister, you had better start learning what maid of honors does because you are it." Theresa became very quiet, and tears ran down her cheeks.

"Okay, Terri, don't do this to me. You are the strong one, remember?"

Between sniffs, Theresa answered, "Oleather, we have gone through so much, and we have made it through thick and thins. I am just so happy to be a part of all this with you. It really makes me feel special."

"Well, news flash, girlfriend, you are special."

"Oleather, I am sorry for doubting you in the beginning. Marvin is a wonderful man, and I can see that he has made you very happy. Nowadays, when I see you, there is a loving glow about you. I wish I had that glow too."

"Don't worry; it'll be alright, you'll see; things will start looking up for you sooner than you know."

"Marvin could not have made a better selection; you are a wonderful person, Oleather."

"Thank you, Terri, so are you. Hey, how are things coming along with the company? You know you are my right-hand girl."

"Things are definitely on the up and up. The book we are currently working on is being bounded, and I am working on the publicity fliers for the bookstores."

"Great! Thanks, Theresa; I will be in the shop tomorrow to help out in any way I can."

"Oleather, would you like a glass of juice or anything to drink?"

"Oh no, thanks, Theresa, I am okay." "Thanks for coming over, Theresa, I really needed to get excited with someone, and I know I could only do that with you, girl." Oleather escorted Theresa to the front door, and they embraced each other once again before saying their goodbyes.

"See you later, girl; I'll call you when I get in."

"Sounds good. See ya, and thanks again."

Marvin was very excited. He thought of the many loose ends that he needed to wrap things up before his permanent departure to Charleston to meet the love of his life. Today was the last day of his job at the Parole office. Marvin had already tied up his loose ends at Southwestern Bell Telephone Company; his last day was Saturday. It was the middle of the week, and Marvin had lots to do before leaving the Parole office. He organized his files and sat in with Mr. Alston. Mr. Alston would be the one designating his clients' files to the new officer taking Marvin's place. It was a long day because Marvin had worked overtime to get things for the next Parole officer.

Marvin decided to call Oleather on his way home from the office. "Hey honey, how are my two favorite people?" Marvin asked Oleather cheerfully.

"We are doing just fine, baby. What are you up to?"

"Well, baby, I was just calling to let you know that I just left the office permanently. I have three days to wrap up my business here in Houston, and I will be meeting you in Charleston on Sunday night for us to start our new life together."

"Oh baby, sometimes I have to pinch myself to make sure that I am not dreaming, and we are finally going to be together for good as a family."

"Well, honey, you are not dreaming. This is the real thing. Listen, I will call you later when I get home to give you all the flight information. I have shipped some of my things, the others I sold." Marvin hesitated before asking Oleather, "Baby, are you ready for me to...."

"Yes, Marvin, yes, I am so ready for you to be here I could scream." Marvin laughed.

"You make me happy, Oleather."

"I can't believe that we will be married." "

Well, believe it. By the way, talking about our wedding, I am not too interested in a huge wedding. After visiting the judge, I figured family members and a few close friends for a small reception at the house. What do you think about that, sweetie?"

"I agree with you, honey, if that's what you want; it is okay with me, especially since I've done the huge wedding before. We can go to the courthouse and exchange our vows."

"Great, see, we are definitely in sync."

"Theresa and my mom will help me plan the entire thing. I wish your mom and dad were here to share this with us. But I understand how working overseas can be a drag for your mom, and I am sure your dad is looking down on us from heaven. We'll send lots of pictures to your mom coupled with a DVD. So, honey, all you have to do is be there."

"I will come with bells on my toes. And, don't you think for one minute you will be running yourself ragged? I'll be there to help in every way I can, okay?"

"Yes, honey, I will not argue with you."

"I love you, Oleather soon-to-be Kenyatta."

"I love you too, soon-to-be husband, goodbye."

"Bye, baby; I'll talk to you soon."

And That's Love

It was Sunday night, and Oleather was anxiously awaiting Marvin's arrival. Marvin had insisted that Oleather not pick him up from the airport. He wanted to take a taxi. Oleather was lying on the couch wearing an oversized white tee shirt. Her hair was cascading over her shoulders, and she was half watching the television and half waiting to hear the doorbell.

Marvin was about two blocks away from the house, and his heart was racing in anticipation. He was ready to see Oleather. Marvin paid the driver and tipped him generously when the taxi pulled in front of Oleather's house. He had with him four suitcases and two handbags. The driver helped him with the bags to the door then left. Marvin rang the doorbell.

Although Oleather was anticipating the doorbell to ring, she almost jumped right out of her skin when it did. "Who is it?" she crooned.

"It's the love of your life," came the reply. Oleather could not open the door fast enough. They embraced each other and kissed passionately until Marvin decided to make the first move to get into the house.

"Welcome home, honey." Oleather greeted.

"It's good to be home Oleather; it's really good to be home."

"Let me help you with some of that," Oleather said, referring to Marvin's luggage.

"Oh, absolutely not! I will not allow you to hurt yourself and our baby."

"Oh, Marvin, I am not handicapped, you know, just a little pregnant."

"Nevertheless, I'll do it. But thanks anyway."

"So, how are you honey, you look great for a pregnant woman."

"Oh, and pregnant women are not supposed to look great?" Oleather asked, bumping Marvin playfully on his hips."

"Hey, watch it, don't want you to...."

"Shhh, kiss me again." After Marvin finally got his luggage in, they sat at the dinner table and talked, touched, and kissed like they hadn't seen each other in years.

"Oleather?"

"Yes, Marvin."

"Marry me tomorrow."

"Let's do it; we'll go to the courthouse and get it done."

"Great, then it's settled. Tomorrow night, we will be officially husband and wife."

"Oooh, Marvin, I do like the sound of that. I will get together with Theresa and my mom, and we'll plan the reception for next

Saturday. We could do a combination of a reception and house warming gathering." Oleather poured Marvin a glass of White Zinfandel to "relax him after his trip," and Marvin could not have been more receptive.

"I now pronounce you husband and wife," the judge said, "you may kiss your bride." Marvin held Oleather and kissed her with pride. Theresa was there to witness the joining of Oleather and Marvin; she could not hold back the tears of joy she felt for her friend. Oleather's mom and dad were very supportive of her marriage, and when she took Marvin to the house, her dad and Marvin hit it off almost immediately. Marvin and Oleather's dad had left to look at Oleather's dad's computer when her mom handed her an envelope. It was a check written out to Mr. & Mrs. Kenyatta. "This honey is for you and your husband's honeymoon. I'd like you to go wherever you'd like and have a wonderful time. Your dad and I are very proud of you. You have done very well for yourself, and this is just a small token to show you how much we support and love you. Oleather's eyes filled with tears as she hugged her mother in admiration. Although Oleather had been busy getting her life together, she still called her parents to let them know she loved them and to let them know what was going on in her life. Oleather was about to make her parents grandparents, and they were pleased about it.

The wedding reception was held at the house, and very close friends and family were there. It was one of the most memorable times for Oleather and Marvin. They were both so visibly happy it seemed to rub off on the people surrounding them. Oleathers favorite catering service catered to the food, and the music was just perfect. Theresa and Oleather's mom did an excellent job at organizing the reception. After everyone left, Oleather and Marvin did not have the energy to do anything but lay in each other's arms and sleep like babies. Marvin woke up the following morning and got out of bed without Oleather's knowledge.

"Wake up, Mrs. Kenyatta; I brought you breakfast." Oleather rolled over to see Marvin holding a tray of scrambled eggs, milk, and apple juice. He even had her prenatal pill in a small container.

"Oh, Marvin, you are a wonderful man. I am so glad I married you."

"Great, then get up and eat up." They had breakfast in bed while watching the news and reminiscing the wonderful evening they had the day before.

"Oleather, where are we going for our honeymoon?"

"I would like to visit Guyana, Marvin. I have heard lots of wonderful things about the country."

"Where is Guyana?"

"It's in South America, very close to Venezuela and Brazil. It's very tropical, and I figured we could go hang out in the beautiful tropical country, lay in a hammock and listen to the parrots and watch the monkeys play in the trees."

"Oooh, Oleather, that sounds wonderful."

Forever Mine

On December 17th, 2002, Oleather and Marvin landed on the airstrip at Guyana's Tehmeri airport; residents traveling home to Guyana cheered as the plane's wheels touched the tarmac. As they got off the plane, Oleather raised her right hand over her eyes to diminish some of the sunlight that seemed to be welcoming them to the country. The airport was a small wooded building, and going through customs was a long and tiring process. Uniformed performers were singing welcoming songs as Oleather and Marvin waited in the customs line. The people were very friendly and seemed so happy and carefree. The crowded airport was hot, and both Oleather and Marvin, although sweaty and tired, were happy to be away from the cold climate.

"Weh you going, sir?" A taxi driver inquired of Marvin.

"We are heading to the Pegasus Hotel," Marvin said, hugging Oleather.

"I can get yuh dere in a jiffy. Is dis yuh first time in Guyana mon?"

"Yes, we are recently married, and we chose your country for our honeymoon." Oleather was enjoying the beautiful greenery around the airport. She could not believe how beautiful and wildly the bougainvilleas and hibiscuses were growing.

"Well, sir, yuh couldn't have chosen a better place to be dis time of de year." He grinned and showed a perfect set of white teeth.

"What's that over there?" Oleather asked, pointing to a group of people hauling some colored drums.

"Oh, dat's de steel ban. Dey gettin' ready to play music. It's beautiful man, I am sure yuh gun get de opportunity to listen to some good steel ban music before yuh go back to America," the driver said as he placed the last piece of luggage in the trunk of the car.

The drive to the hotel was beautiful. Because it was 2:30 in the afternoon, they could do some sightseeing as they traveled. Marvin and Oleather were amazed at the vendors positioned at the side of the streets with small colorful "stands" selling mangoes, coconuts, guavas, and vegetables. Kids were selling parrots and other birds in cages which Oleather and Marvin found out they had caught; that was how they made extra "pocket change." "By the way, meh name is Otis," said the driver, "I gun give yuh meh numba so yuh could call me mon fuh anything, anything at all. Try not to be too trusting to people here though, de country sweet, but it got it good and bad."

"Thanks, Otis," Marvin said.

"I'm getting hungry," Oleather said, "can we stop to get something to eat?"

"Sure, nat a problem, mon, we could stop wen we get to de city of Georgetown."

The city of Georgetown was busy. People were hustling and bustling about the crowded streets going about their businesses. Christmas was in the air as colorful ornaments and decorations could be seen in the showcases of local stores; Santa clauses were even in the streets shaking bells encouraging shoppers to donate money for different fundraisers. There were vendors selling anything from turtles to iguanas tied by the legs to keep them from escaping.

"Why are they selling turtles?" Oleather asked.

"Oh, it's a delicacy," replied Otis, "People cook dem in a curry sauce. It's good stuff, and yuh should try it before yuh go back home."

Oleather almost gagged. "Really, it's okay; I am sure there are some other delicacies we could try." Otis laughed a hearty and contagious laugh, and Marvin joined him. There were vendors with baskets on their heads calling out, "come and get yuh fresh fish here." People were rushing to taxis and minibusses in what seemed like attempts to get where they were going in a hurry. There were street shows, and loud reggae and calypso music could be heard at just about every other corner. The city was very colorful, and the historical-looking wooden buildings were impressive.

"Marvin, this is really different. I like this." Oleather said. Marvin hugged her and kissed her in admiration of his new bride.

After inquiring about what Oleather and Marvin felt like eating, they stopped at a local Kentucky Fried Chicken. To Oleather and Marvin's surprise, the chicken was seasoned differently, and they loved the flavor.

"So far, so good," Marvin mused. They finished lunch and were then taken to the Pegasus Hotel. The driver handed his business card to Marvin and wished them a wonderful visit to Guyana. They made arrangements for him to pick them up to take them back to the airport. Otis' eyes opened wide when he received his payment and a nice tip from Marvin.

"Thank you, mon, you a good mon. See you on Saturday morning." Hotel personnel assisted Oleather and Marvin with their luggage as they checked in.

The room was absolutely beautiful. Oleather and Marvin had a view of the Demerara River from their balcony, and tropical birds could be seen below, flying and playing in the trees in a carefree manner. The birds were like a welcoming committee below the balcony. Oleather felt peaceful and excited all in one. They decided to shower and "take a load off."

"Baby, we haven't had a chance to exchange any loving since we've been here." At that moment, there was a knock on their room door.

"Room service" was the voice on the other side.

"But we didn't order room service," Marvin said to Oleather. Reluctantly, Marvin opened the door. A young man in his early to mid-twenties gave Marvin a basket filled with local rum and fruit.

"Welcome to Guyana, and welcome to the Pegasus hotel. We hope you enjoy your stay. If you need anything at all, please call the number listed by the phone."

"Thanks," Marvin said, surprised, "that's very nice." Marvin hung a "do not disturb" sign outside the door and locked the door.

"This time is ours, baby. Welcome to our honeymoon." Marvin held Oleather close, and they kissed passionately. They showered and could not keep their hands off each other. Oleather and Marvin made love repeatedly to the reggae love songs that blared into their room from the bands playing at the seawall. They could not have been a happier couple.

During the following days, Oleather and Marvin visited the museum, visited the zoo, and did lots of shopping. Oleather especially loved the times they spent at the beach and the hotel's pool. Tropical plants and the constant singing of birds frequently surrounded them. The days seemed to go by very fast.

"Baby, I can't believe that we will be returning home tomorrow already."

"I know; it seems like we just got here. I was beginning to enjoy myself. The people are great."

"I agree, Marvin. What do you say? Let's go to the beach and make this the best day ever." Oleather hugged Marvin around the waist as she looked deeply into his eyes."

"Sure, baby, let's do." It was a beautiful Friday midday. Although the sun was scorching, it was the perfect day to go for a swim at the beach.

The water was lovely and inviting, and Oleather and Marvin held hands as they ran into the water like two happy-go-lucky children without a care in the world. There weren't too many people at the beach, and Oleather decided she really would make this moment memorable.

"Marvin?"

"Yes, baby."

"Come closer to me." Marvin moved closer to Oleather. She cupped his face in her hands and kissed him so passionately that the bulge in his pants became noticeable. Marvin and Oleather were the only two people in the water, at that beach, in Guyana at that time. They were so far out in the water that it did not even matter because they could not be seen. They had found some huge rocks and made it their fortress. Marvin took off Oleather's two-piece, and Oleather undressed Marvin. Looking into Oleather's beautiful brown eyes, Marvin could not believe the moment.

"You have made me the happiest man in the world Mrs. Oleather Kenyatta."

"Yeah? And I am the luckiest woman there is." Oleather was filled with desire as Marvin eased his way into her first slowly, then faster and faster. Oleather wrapped her legs around Marvin's thighs giving him more ease to keep his rhythm going.

"Oh, Marvin, don't stop," Oleather said as she dug her nails into Marvin's back.

"Never, my love, never." Marvin continued to pump his manhood into Oleather's warmness until they both reached the most powerful climax they ever met. Shaking and rocking, Marvin released Oleather's legs.

"Wow! That was awesome." Oleather said in between gasps.

"You could say that again. I will never forget this." They got dressed and started back to the shore when Oleather told Marvin to wait.

"I have something I want to give you." Oleather waded out of the water, her tummy barely showing that she was pregnant. Marvin decided to do a little splashing of his own. Oleather returned with a piece of paper she had left under her towel. "I wrote this for you, baby, and I hope you like it."

Had I Only Known

Had I only known
that a man so smart,
would come along,
and touch my lonely heart;
Man, you are sweet.
Had I only known
that your strength would
become my knight,
and shining armor;
Man, you are strong.
Had I only known
that your confidence in me
would help me feel emotionally secure;
Man, you are so caring.
Had I only known
that you would become
my husband and best friend;
Man, you make me happy.

The End!

About the Author

Dadisi Mwende Netifnet, born Marvin Leroy Alston, in Charleston, South Carolina. Through the years, he has been in an intense struggle to improve his art of writing. He has read his poetry in many cities throughout the United States and Canada. He has also read his poetry in many different countries worldwide, such as Egypt, Senegal, Gambia and Freeport, Grand Bahamas. In 2002, Dadisi was awarded the Shakespeare Trophy of Excellence and the 2002 Poet of the Year Gold Medallion by the Famous Poets Society. Dadisi resides in Houston, Heartland. Look for him at area poetry readings, arrange for him to read to your group, or get one or all of his publications for your library. You will be uplifted and delighted.

Other Books Written by Author

Additional books by Dadisi Mwende Netifnet, aka Marvin Leroy Alston

Poetry for Today's Young Black Revolutionary Minds
Need I Say More?
Love Flows Like the River
Think with Your Spiritual Mind

www.ingramcontent.com/pod-product-compliance
Lightning Source LLC
LaVergne TN
LVHW091550060526
838200LV00036B/783